Is Finn Cheating on Elizabeth?

"Last night I saw Finn with some blond chick," Sam said. "He was all over her. I thought you should know before your date with him tonight."

Elizabeth let out a short, dry laugh. "Yeah, right, Sam."

He ran his hands through his sandy-brown hair. "Liz, Finn's a two-timing jerk. And you'd better wake up to that fact before it's too late."

"Too late for what?" Elizabeth snapped back. Had Sam overheard her telling Jessica that Finn was pressuring her to sleep with him?

"You know what I'm talking about, Wakefield."

So he had heard. She felt her stomach sink with that knowledge, but she wasn't going to let Sam and his jealous lies get to her.

Not tonight.

Bantam Books in the Sweet Valley University series.
Ask your bookseller for the books you have missed.

And don't miss these Sweet Valley University Thriller Editions:

Visit the Official Sweet Valley Web Site on the Internet at:

http://www.sweetvalley.com

SWEET VALLEY UNIVERSITY®

The First Time

Written by
Laurie John

Created by
FRANCINE PASCAL

BANTAM BOOKS
NEW YORK · TORONTO · LONDON · SYDNEY · AUCKLAND

RL: 8, AGES 014 AND UP

THE FIRST TIME
A Bantam Book / February 2000

*Sweet Valley High® and Sweet Valley University®
are registered trademarks of Francine Pascal.
Conceived by Francine Pascal.*

Produced by 17th Street Productions, Inc.
33 West 17th Street
New York, NY 10011.

ISBN: 0-553-49307-8

Visit us on the Web! www.randomhouse.com/teens

Published simultaneously in the United States and Canada

*Bantam Books is an imprint of Random House Children's Books, a
division of Random House, Inc. BANTAM BOOKS and the rooster
colophon are registered trademarks of Random House, Inc. Bantam Books,
1540 Broadway, New York, New York 10036.*

PRINTED IN THE UNITED STATES OF AMERICA

OPM   0 9 8 7 6 5 4 3 2 1

To Susan Johansson

Chapter
One

"Elizabeth Wakefield is *not* my type," Sam Burgess repeated to his friend Bugsy Frieman over the loud buzz of voices and music in Frankie's. "She's a total shrew. And shut up already, man—you're messing with my concentration."

Dart poised in his hand, Sam squinted, zeroing in on the bull's-eye of the dartboard six feet in front of him.

"Uh-huh," Bugsy replied, leaning against the wall next to Sam with a mug of beer in one hand and a chicken wing in the other. "You're not into Elizabeth. That's why you talk about her all the time. That's why you're living with her."

Sam turned to Bugsy and aimed the dart at his friend's tie-dyed chest. "I moved into her off-campus house because I couldn't find any other place and school was starting the next day. And it's not like

1

Wakefield and I are sharing a room. We're two flights and two other housemates apart. So go eat another chicken wing or something, okay?"

"Whatever you say, dude." With a smirk Bugsy snatched another psycho-hot wing from the double order they'd gotten delivered to Frankie's.

That was just one of the reasons why Sam liked hanging out at Frankie's, which was far off the beaten path. The small nightclub didn't serve food, but Rita, the cool manager, let you order in whatever you wanted as long as you didn't leave a mess. The other reason Frankie's was so cool was that the girls were cute (including the waitresses), the beer was cheap, the DJ had a clue, and Sam never saw anyone from SVU—or, as his friends at Orange County College called it, SV-Useless— hanging out there.

Sam plucked a wing from the basket and devoured it. Man, that was hot! He took a swig of beer, wiped his fingers on a napkin, then squinted at the dartboard again. He threw the dart and watched it strike the exact spot he was aiming for: triple 17.

"Awesome, dude," Bugsy said, nodding his respect.

Sam thought darts was the ultimate sport. It required skill, strategy, and nerves of steel, yet you barely had to lift a finger to play the game. Which was the ultimate metaphor for how Sam liked to live his life.

Too bad relationships aren't more like darts, he mused. Dealing with girls like Elizabeth required skill and strategy too, but *they* demanded everything you had inside you.

"Lots of babes here tonight," Bugsy commented as he looked around the hopping nightclub and gnawed on another chicken wing. "Whoa, dude—check *that* out!"

Sam followed the direction of Bugsy's lusty stare. The surfer-slash-stoner-slash-OCC philosophy major had good taste, Sam thought, eyeing the blonde who had his friend's tongue hanging out of his mouth. The girl wasn't a "townie," though. Sam could spot SVU in a chick a mile away.

"And sitting all alone, waiting for me to go over and keep her company," Bugsy added, wagging his eyebrows. "I'll be back with a phone number in ten minutes."

Sam blocked Bugsy's way with his arm. "Don't waste your ego. She's with a date. Check out her table—there's a half-full wineglass in front of her and another next to her. Guy's probably in the bathroom or something. And, uh, no offense, buddy, but you can't eat, like, a hundred psycho-hot wings and chat up some girl without first brushing your teeth or popping a mint."

3

Bugsy cupped his hand around his mouth, pulled it away, then sniffed it and nodded. "All the babes are taken!" he complained, slamming his picked-clean chicken-wing bone on the floor.

"Pick it up, man," boomed an I-mean-business voice from behind them. "And if I see you throw one more bone on the floor, you're outta here."

Sam turned around to see Todd Wilkins, wearing a Frankie's baseball cap, glaring from Bugsy to the offending chicken bone.

"*You* work here?" Sam asked, surprised that Wilkins *(a)* worked in a bar and *(b)* worked in one this far off campus and frequented by locals instead of SVU snots like himself.

"Yeah, *I* work here," Todd replied. "I'm the back-bar guy, so it's my job to keep this place clean."

"Chill, dude, I'm picking it up," Bugsy muttered, leaning down to snatch the wing. "Hey, so why do you work here and not some place closer to SV-Useless?"

Todd cracked up with laughter and slapped Bugsy on the shoulder. "You just earned yourself the right to throw as many wings on the floor as you want. *Useless* is right, man. The people that go there are just a bunch of phony snobs who think they're better than everyone. I work here because I like this place, and I live only a few miles from here."

4

Sam stared at him, shocked *and* impressed. As Todd raced off at the sound of a glass shattering on the floor, Sam shook his head in wonder. He had to give the guy credit. Maybe Wilkins was cooler than Sam had thought when he'd met him over the summer on that cross-country road-trip contest. The very one during which Sam had met Elizabeth.

"Man, I cannot stop staring at that blond chick's knockers!" Bugsy exclaimed, his eyes popping out of his head.

Sam turned around, expecting to catch an eyeful of an attractively filled out sweater, but this time a guy was sitting with the blonde and blocking Sam's view. "See, Bugs, told you—"

The rest of Sam's sentence died in his throat when the blonde's date turned to signal the waitress.

It was Finn Robinson, Dr. Cool. The cheesy med student who Elizabeth was dating. *Obsessing over is more like it,* Sam thought bitterly, *including whether or not to have sex with him.* Sam had caught that tidbit while eavesdropping on a conversation Elizabeth was having with her twin sister, Jessica.

He watched as Finn, who according to Elizabeth was the *ideal* boyfriend, fondled his date's thigh. Blondie snaked her arms around Dr. Cool's neck and trailed kisses across his lying, cheating face.

5

Sam thought he might throw up every chicken wing he'd eaten as Robinson pulled a stethoscope from his knapsack and flirtatiously positioned it on the girl's enormous chest while he listened to her heart.

"Sam, you okay, man?" Bugsy asked. "You look like you're gonna be sick or something. Too many wings?"

Sam shook his head. "That guy over there with the blonde. He's a med student at SVU, and he's supposed to be in love with a girl I know. A girl who wouldn't be too happy to know he's playing doctor with some babe."

"No way would a med student at SVU bring a date way out here to a bar full of townies," Bugsy said. "Probably just looks like him."

It's Huckleberry Finn Robinson, all right. Sam was sure. And of course the jerk would bring a date all the way out here. Robinson wouldn't be stupid enough to risk getting caught with another girl around campus; Elizabeth or one of her friends might spot him. Sam could just imagine Finn telling his date it would be *fun* to go slumming with the townies, like an event in itself.

And what Sam also knew for sure—what he felt so hard and deep in his gut, he'd bet his life on it—was that Finn Robinson was going after Elizabeth because she was a virgin: She was

6

nothing more than a conquest. Once Finn had her, he'd dump her faster than she could say, *But you told me you loved me. . . .*

You're busted now, Huckleberry, Sam thought, downing the last of his beer. Now he had to figure out the best way to share this unappetizing news with Elizabeth. It wasn't like he wanted to rub it in her face, even though it proved he'd been right about Finn all along.

All that mattered was that she dumped the two-timing sleaze.

Elizabeth Wakefield stared at herself in the mirror on the living-room wall as she waited for Finn to arrive. *Too much?* she wondered, taking in the glossy, pinkish brown lipstick, the upswept hair, and the little black dress.

No. Just right, she assured herself. *You don't want to look like some unsophisticated undergrad who doesn't have a clue. You want to look . . .*

How did she want to look? Not too sexy, that was for sure. Dressing Jessica-hot had worked a little too well in capturing Finn's interest during their handful of dates, Elizabeth thought, her palms getting clammier by the second.

Finn wanted to advance their relationship to the bedroom. He'd made that very clear during their last two dates. And Elizabeth had made it embarrassingly clear that she wasn't ready.

But if Finn *was* the one—and Elizabeth was almost sure he was—then maybe she *was* ready. Was. Wasn't. Was. Wasn't.

Arrrgh! she thought. Why was this so confusing? How did you know when you *were* ready? When Elizabeth had confided in her sister about Finn's subtle pressure, Jessica had told her to stop worrying, that the way to keep Finn's interest was *not* to sleep with him! Keep him wanting more, Jessica had assured her.

But what if I make him wait too long? Elizabeth wondered, gnawing on her lower lip. What if she was never ready? Would he still go out with her, or would he dump her for a girl who would sleep with him?

If he really loves you . . . Yeah, yeah. Elizabeth knew intellectually that if Finn really cared deeply for her, he'd wait. But at the same time it didn't seem wrong for him to want or even expect a physical aspect to their relationship. They weren't in high school, after all. She was a sophomore in college, and he was a med student.

Elizabeth's heart skipped a beat when she heard Finn's footsteps on the stairs outside. But instead of the chiming bell, the sound of a frantic key turning the lock was followed by the door whooshing open and Sam rushing in. *Great,* thought Elizabeth, *instead of Prince Charming, I get the king of sarcastic remarks.*

8

Sam stared at her for a second, then tossed his knapsack and two textbooks on the sofa. "So I overheard you telling Neil you had a date with Dr. Cool tonight, and—"

Elizabeth rolled her eyes. "So and *nothing*, Sam. It's none of your business." Nothing in her personal life would ever be Sam Burgess's business again. After their brief fling last summer Elizabeth had vowed never to let him hurt her again. Never to let him that close again. "And stop calling him Dr. Cool. It's annoying."

He jammed his hands in his pockets. "*So and* I gave up a chance to play hoops to bust my butt to get home before you left for your date. There's something I have to tell you, Wakefield."

"Well, I'd talk fast if I were you. Finn will be here any minute."

"Speaking of Dr. Cool," he began, "I saw him last night."

"So?"

"I saw him at Frankie's, the bar downtown where I go to play darts. He was with this blond chick, and he was all over her. I thought you should know."

Elizabeth let out a short, dry laugh. "Yeah, right, Sam."

He ran his hands through his sandy brown hair. "Liz, he's a two-timing jerk. And you'd better wake up to that fact before it's too late."

"Too late for *what?*" Elizabeth snapped back. *Had* Sam overheard her telling Jessica that Finn was pressuring her to sleep with him?

"You *know* what I'm talking about, Wakefield."

So he *had* heard. She felt her stomach sink with that knowledge, but she wasn't going to let Sam get to her. Not tonight. "Sam, you've done nothing but diss Finn since I started seeing him. You're just jealous of him, and you should start waking up to *that* fact. And next time pick a more believable bar. Finn would never take a girl to the neighborhood Frankie's is in. Give me a break."

"That's exactly why he *did* take a date there," Sam fired back. "Because he figured he wouldn't get caught. Think about it, Wakefield. Why would I bother making this up?"

Elizabeth glared at him. "I don't know why you do anything you do, Sam."

Sam opened his mouth to retort, but the doorbell rang. As he brushed past her to his bedroom, he looked her straight in the eye and said, "Just be careful."

"Welcome to Theta house, pledges!" Jessica Wakefield announced from the podium in the sorority's elegant meeting room.

Chloe Murphy darted a smile at her best friend, Val Berger, who sat in the folding chair beside her. *Here we go,* Chloe thought, glancing

10

down the list of pledge requirements in her hand. *Val and I will fulfill every one, and by next week we'll be full-fledged Thetas!*

"During pledge week," Jessica continued, smiling at the twenty girls seated in a straight row before her, "you must fulfill every requirement, or you will be eliminated. And you must perform any task that a Theta sister asks of you. The rules and regulations of pledge week are listed at the back of your packets. Read them carefully."

Val reached across Chloe's lap to point to number seven on the list of requirements. "'Kiss a Sigma on the lips upon command by a Theta sister,'" Val read in a horrified whisper. "I could never just go up to a strange guy and kiss him. What if the guy doesn't want me to?"

Chloe was trying to pay attention to Jessica and didn't want to get in trouble for whispering with another pledge. But Chloe knew that Val needed extra encouragement. The girl had been a mousy nerd before Chloe had taken her under her wing right before rush week had started. It was thanks to Chloe that Val had even made it here. Chloe had gotten her a makeover and taken her shopping (financing it herself since Val was so broke), and now Val looked great. But a physical change wasn't enough, apparently. Val would need plenty of support if she was going to make it through pledge week alive.

11

"Val, look at you," Chloe whispered. "Any guy would want you to go up to him and kiss him! Don't worry."

"I appreciate you saying that, Chlo, but c'mon—what does kissing some guy have to do with joining a sorority?" Val demanded under her breath. "I thought Theta had changed from its snarky, mean-spirited ways."

Chloe gave Val a harsh look and whispered back, "It *has* changed. Theta isn't the vicious sorority it used to be."

"I know," Val said. "I'm just a little nervous. Everyone was really nice during rush week."

Well, not everyone, Chloe thought, recalling the endless parties she and Val had gone to. They'd spent days sucking up to the most undeserving Thetas when the only sisters Chloe had cared about impressing were the big cheeses: Jessica and her best friends, the girls who made up the Theta government.

"So stop worrying," Chloe whispered. "Pledge week is about showing your commitment to Theta, and being forced to kiss a Sigma isn't exactly torture. But most important, do you want to be a Theta or not?"

Val nodded. "More than anything. You know that."

"So we're in this together?" Chloe asked.

Val's smile got even wider. "Together."

Chloe nodded and turned her attention back to Jessica. Finally everything was working out. By becoming a Theta, Chloe would single-handedly save her freshman year, which so far had been absolutely horrible. Chloe had a friend now, a best friend, and soon she'd have a ton of instant friends in her sisters. That's all Chloe had ever wanted.

And nothing would stand in her way. Certainly not some stupid, embarrassing pledge requirements. She would do whatever she had to do to make sure she became a Theta Alpha Theta sister. After all, Chloe was well used to humiliation.

Chapter Two

Elizabeth couldn't take her eyes off Finn's perfect face as he sat across from her in the romantic Italian restaurant just off campus. She knew she had a goofy smile on her own face as he continued with his funny story about his anatomy instructor's pathetic taste in clashing plaid outfits.

Elizabeth wanted to record every moment of tonight into memory. Every detail. The way Finn's strong hands rested on the tablecloth, his arms and chest clad in a gray cashmere jacket. The waiter in black tie laying plates and dishes on the table and clearing them away. The savor of every dish, the gooey eggplant and the lighter manicotti, the unusual vinaigrette on the salad, the fine, smooth red wine that felt like it danced on her tongue. The bread and butter. The shape of the ice cubes in the water glasses. The conversation, every word.

That he'd been named after a man named Augustus Finn who'd saved his grandmother's life. That he dreamed of moving to a small coastal town where he could be a country doctor and paint in the hours between sundown and darkness.

Every word, every sight and sound, went into her memory, carefully cataloged. *Rainbow in prism made by cut-glass goblet. Aroma of cheese, garlic, white wine, clams. Finn's fingertips in my palm. Tickle. Dry mouth, don't want to move hand to reach for wineglass.*

She fantasized about living in a beautiful California coastal town, in a house on the ocean where she could write and gaze out over the Pacific cliffs. She imagined Finn on the deck, painting the seascape before dinner, a loose straw hat on his head above a roll-neck sweater and faded jeans. She was preparing manicotti stuffed with cheese, their favorite dinner.

He's the one, she realized with absolutely certainty.

I saw him all over a girl at Frankie's. . . .

Elizabeth froze. How had Sam's jealous lies possibly managed to invade her mind at this moment, the moment she'd been waiting for: the moment she *knew?*

Just forget it, she ordered herself. *Sam is lying.*

16

"Elizabeth?" Finn asked. "See anything you like?"

She'd been so lost in her thoughts that she hadn't even noticed the amazing selection of desserts the waiter had wheeled over on a cart.

Why was she wasting her precious time thinking about that slacker anyway?

"Hmmm . . . ," she whispered. "Everything looks amazing. Why don't you surprise me, Finn? We can share something, maybe."

He smiled and ordered two cappuccinos, one cannoli, and two forks. Then he took her hand in his, caressing her palm and gazing into her eyes. *He's the one. . . .*

By the time they'd finished the cannoli, spooning each other bites and laughing between more warm, funny stories about themselves, Elizabeth had forgotten she was in a restaurant surrounded by people. It was as if she and Finn were the only two people in the world.

He moved his chair slightly to her side of the table, then wrapped both his hands around hers. She could feel his warm breath on her neck as he leaned closer to her.

"There's something I want to tell you. And something I want to ask you," Finn whispered in her ear.

Her ear was tingling.

"Elizabeth, I feel like I'm falling in love with you."

17

Her heart skipped a beat. *Love! Am I dreaming?* she wondered, wishing she could pinch herself without looking stupid. She could feel his breath on her ear and her neck, and her heart began to accelerate and pound in her chest.

She opened her mouth to speak, but no words would come out. All she could think was: *He's in love with me. And I'm in love with him!*

"Elizabeth," Finn whispered.

That's my name, she thought. *That's me. This isn't a dream.*

"I want our relationship to be exclusive." Finn held her hands more tightly. "I hope you do too."

Her throat was clamped shut tight.

He gave her hand a squeeze. "Do you?"

Elizabeth rested her temple on Finn's forehead. She could feel her eyes growing hot and wet. She paused briefly in her pleasure to blink them—and her remaining shred of doubt—away.

"Yes, Finn," she whispered. "I do. Very much so. And I think I'm falling in love with you too."

Finn leaned forward to kiss her. She felt all her blood rush to her head, her heartbeat pulsing madly, the rest of the world falling away.

"Let's go somewhere we can be alone," he whispered. "I want to be alone with you right now so bad—" He paused, gazing into her eyes with a very serious expression. "I'm sorry, Elizabeth. I'm pressuring you again, and that's not what I want

18

to do. If you're still not ready, that's okay. We'll just snuggle—"

"I'm ready," she told him, gazing into those caramel-colored eyes. "I'm very ready."

Nina Harper bobbed her head to the pulsing rhythm of the bass drum as she stared transfixed at one of the most gorgeous guys she'd ever laid eyes on.

His light brown skin glistened with sweat in the spotlight. She drank in the sight of him, from the flowing black dreadlocks that framed his sculpted face, all the way down his awe-inspiring body. Nina's eyes lingered on his bare torso.

She moved closer to the stage to get closer to the sight of that body. That face. The sound of his voice. A vocal mix of Lenny Kravitz and Eddie Vedder. The lead singer, alternating between soothing crooning and guttural howls. The way he worked his leather-clad hips in tune to the outrageous guitar solos. His infectious smile.

Finally Nina caught his eye. And from that moment he was singing only to her. *"You. You're the one I want. You."*

Nina knew it was just the chorus of a song, but for a fleeting spell it felt like he was speaking to her. He held her gaze until the song was over, ending with a sexy raised eyebrow before he turned to grab a bottle of spring water from the drum riser. She watched as he gulped the pure, clear liquid and proceeded to cool himself down with a refreshing squirt to the top of his head. He shook himself dry, his frenetic dreads casting a mist of water mixed with sweat that tickled Nina's face in the front row.

"Xavier's pretty hot, huh?"

So that's his name, Nina thought, pleased as she turned to face Francesca, her newest friend from SVU. Francesca's sort-of boyfriend Billy played drums for Wired, and she was the one who had invited Nina here to Starlights nightclub to see them play.

But the past few times she'd been here, Nina hadn't even gotten near the stage to pay attention to the band. She'd been too busy freaking out that she was in a nightclub on a school night. Getting checked out by guys for the first time in her life. Getting home past a reasonable hour.

When she looked back up at the band, Xavier was eyeing her once again. Or was it just her imagination?

"He sure is checking *you* out!" Francesca shouted in her ear.

Unbelievable, Nina thought, grinning at her friend. Just last week she'd been boring old Nina Harper, studying physics on a Saturday night. Now she was the new and improved Nina, in another borrowed sexy outfit from Francesca, swaying to a

20

rock band and being checked out by a hot lead singer.

I should be studying for my calculus exam, she told herself, taking a brief peek at her watch. The last time she'd gone out to Starlights with Francesca, she'd yawned all the next day through her classes, then slept through her alarm and missed work at the lab.

But Xavier's molecules are so much more interesting . . . , she thought. *Stay one more hour, then go home and hit the books. You deserve tonight, girl!*

Elizabeth slid into the passenger seat of Finn's Saab, which was cold beneath her short black dress. As he walked behind the car to the driver's side, she felt the state of reverie she had experienced in the restaurant subside to the cold automotive reality. She took a deep breath and peered through the windshield at the stars. The night was very clear and quiet.

This is it, she thought. *Finn will drive us to his apartment, and before the night is over, we'll . . .*

He told you he loves you. He told you he wants to be with only you. What more could you want? How much readier do you need to be?

Finn whisked himself into the car, closed the door, and put the key in the ignition. He paused, his eyes fixed on the ignition, then he turned to face her. "Elizabeth, this is the beginning of something incredible, I promise."

"I know it is—" She paused, biting her lip, and placed her hands on the sides of the leather bucket seat. Her palms suddenly felt damp, and she clasped the hem of her dress. Finn took her hands in his and squeezed them, then leaned closer until their faces were just inches apart.

He kissed her. She held herself very still as her mouth softened in his and then kissed him back hotly, turning her body to meet his embrace. He grasped her waist and lifted her toward him so that her upper body rested against his. She slipped her hands around his neck. They kissed furiously, clutching each other.

Then Finn moved his hand lower, lower, and lower still. Elizabeth stiffened. She felt his warm hand reaching up her thigh to the edge of her panties.

Oh, no, she thought. *This couldn't be what he meant by "going somewhere we can be alone."* Could it? They were in a parking lot!

She squirmed away. "Finn," she said. "Don't."

"What's the matter?" he asked. "We're finally alone."

"No, we're not," she replied. "We're in the middle of a parking lot."

"No one can see us," he protested, drawing her chin up to kiss her again. "C'mon. I just can't resist you."

He kissed her again, and she felt the pleasant warmth of her passion extend from her lips down to the pit of her stomach. *If he weren't such a good kisser, I wouldn't be in this mess,* she thought. But she didn't want to stop.

He held her firmly against him, his kiss deepening, his hands roving up and down her back, her sides. Then he caressed her more gently, his hand lingering on her thigh. Slowly his fingers inched up and up and up until they again rested on the edge of her underwear.

And again her desire turned to fear. She leaned back from him and stared into his eyes. "Finn, please," she whispered. "I—I . . . not here. Not like this."

Finn looked a little surprised but moved his hand to the small of her back. Elizabeth sat up, repositioned herself in her seat, and guided Finn's wayward leg back to his side of the car.

They sat silently for a moment. She turned to see the starry sky, but the windows were starting to get fogged up.

What am I supposed to say? she wondered. *Should I say something? Should he?*

She was grateful when he started the car. Elizabeth flipped the heater to defogger, and they took off down the road. At least they were moving, doing something other than sitting awkwardly.

"I'm sorry, Liz," he told her, his eyes on the dark street in front of him. "Once again I got a little crazy. What you do to me . . ."

She sent him a tentative smile. She liked that he wanted her, desired her. And he had apologized. She really had nothing to be upset about. It was just a make-out session gone too far in a car. *Big deal*, she told herself. After all, how many times had Todd Wilkins tried to get past first base in his dad's BMW back in Sweet Valley High's parking lot?

"It's okay, Finn," she told him, resting her hand on his shoulder. He briefly glanced at her and smiled, and she felt satisfied with the strength of their bond. Everything was going to be fine.

Her hair had come partway down, and she pulled it the rest of the way out of its pins. Then she turned off the heater and powered down her window, reveling in the cool evening breeze whipping through her hair. This was how she wanted to be: free and herself, driving down the California winding road with the guy she loved.

"So what do you say we watch one of those classic old movies you love so much?" Finn suggested, deftly handling the Saab around a curve. "I have a collection of them, and we can nuke some popcorn and just cozy up on the couch."

"That sounds great," she told him, her palms suddenly getting sweaty again.

It was what would happen *after* the video that made her so nervous. If she couldn't handle a little groping in a car, could she handle anything in the privacy of his own bedroom?

Chapter Three

The crowd erupted in applause as Wired's electrifying show ended. Nina was still riveted to the front of the stage, transfixed by the sight of Xavier as he took a final bow and disappeared behind the curtain.

"Come with me!" Francesca grabbed Nina's hand. "Let's go backstage and hang with the band. You've got to meet Xavier before all the groupies start descending."

"I don't know," Nina said. "I really should get back to the dorm. I've got a major calc exam tomorrow."

Francesca rolled her eyes. "Nina, you *do* want to meet him, don't you? You couldn't keep your eyes off him their whole set."

"Yes, but . . ." Nina hesitated.

"But what?" Francesca demanded. "Xavier's

worth risking a C on a stupid calculus test. And I'm sure he wants to meet you too."

Nina looked at Francesca, with her long, black hair and cool clothes. Nina could see why one of the guys in Wired would want to go out with Francesca, but what about her? What did boring, bookish Nina have to offer, even in the sexy mini-skirt and tight shirt she'd borrowed from Francesca?

"C'mon," Francesca said, plunging into the surrounding sea of bodies. Nina followed her around the stage toward the restricted area, carefully weaving between and around people. She was extra careful not to upset a carelessly held drink or get burned by an errant cigarette. Nina couldn't believe how packed Starlights was for a Monday night.

So this is what I've been missing all those nights cooped up in the library, studying for math and science tests, Nina thought as she navigated through the crowd. Nina felt like she was emerging from a cocoon. Stretching her dormant wings for the first time after plodding along for way too long as a slow, studious caterpillar. A boring bookworm. That's what she had been. Maybe she was ready to float and soar like a butterfly.

As she made her way through the crowd, Nina concentrated on following Francesca. Following her advice too. *Francesca's right,* Nina decided. *I do need to loosen up and relax. Go with the flow. Let life take me places.*

But do I really want a C on that calc test? Not really.

Before she had a chance to properly weigh her options, Francesca had stopped in front of a closed door.

Nina looked up at the door and saw a small, gold star with the words *Staff Only* written below it. Behind the door Nina could picture Xavier, toweling the sweat off his awesome physique and—could it be?—happy to meet her. The mental image was enough to make Nina's dilemma disappear.

Forget studying for the calculus test, she told herself. *There's no way I'm leaving now!*

Elizabeth followed Finn into his apartment in the med-student dorms, her palms only slightly sweaty. He switched on the light, then dimmed it romantically and smiled at her. She smiled back.

They'd watch a classic, feed each other popcorn, snuggle, kiss a little. . . . And if she was ready to go further, she would. If she wasn't, Finn would understand. Right?

Satisfied with that, Elizabeth sat on the sofa in his living room while Finn switched on the television and VCR in the armoire facing the leather sofa. He opened one of the cabinets and peered inside, moving things around.

"This is so weird," he said. "I can't find my box of videotapes." He knelt down and dug through the stuffed cabinet, then stood up and looked around the living room, his expression puzzled. "It doesn't seem to be anywhere. Do you mind if we just watch something on TV?"

"That's fine," she said. "Maybe there's an old movie on."

He sat down next to her, his thigh touching hers.

"You're so beautiful," he whispered, kissing her softly once.

She smiled, feeling the warmth spreading through her entire body.

"You're absolutely perfect." He nuzzled her cheek with his and kissed her temple. "Those incredible aqua eyes." A kiss on her earlobe. "That silky blond hair." A kiss on her neck. "That killer dress." A kiss on her jaw. "That killer body." Another on the lips.

She tucked her legs underneath her and reached down to undo the straps on her heels. She didn't want to get them stuck in Finn's leather couch.

Finn reached down to grasp her hand. "No," he murmured. "Leave them on. They're so sexy."

Elizabeth blushed and giggled on his lips. They

kissed slowly but passionately. She wrapped her arms around his shoulders. Without his jacket the muscles of his back were smooth beneath her hands. She slid her hands back and forth on them, enjoying the sensation.

"Elizabeth," he whispered as he lifted her onto his lap, her shoes barely resting on the floor. With her arms around his broad torso she clung tightly to him, kissing him madly. Again she felt her insides give way, as if she were melting.

Finn wrapped his arms around her waist and eased her gently down to lie beneath him on the couch, their kisses unstopping. Their bodies sank down into the soft leather cushions, deeper and deeper.

"Ow!" she cried as something sharp stabbed her from behind.

"What?" Finn asked, startled as he jumped off her. "What's wrong?"

Elizabeth reached between the cushions of the couch. She retrieved a videotape case, which had been poking her very suddenly and sharply in the derriere. Instantly she burst into peals of hysterical laughter.

"Found what you'd been looking for!" she announced. *And not a minute too soon,* she thought. How had things gotten so hot so fast again? If she hadn't been stabbed in the butt by the case, would she have stopped him anyway?

"But," he said in a sensual tone, sitting back down next to her, "maybe we could continue what we were doing and *then* watch one of them."

"Oooh," she chirped, peering into the case, very aware that Finn was staring at her. "You have *High Noon*!"

"Oh, but that's a Western," Finn said. "An old shoot-'em-up cowboy flick. Not very romantic."

But Elizabeth didn't care what they watched. She was simply relieved to have something to do other than make out. "Let's watch it," she said. *I need a little more time to compose myself,* she thought. *Just a little longer.* She studied the videotape box. The film was eighty-five minutes long. *That's almost an hour and a half,* Elizabeth thought. *That ought to be enough to get back to feeling normal.*

"Okay," Finn said, smiling at her. "Movie, it is. You put it in, and I'll get the popcorn going."

In five minutes he was back, bowl of microwave popcorn on the coffee table. Relieved, Elizabeth took off her shoes, and they snuggled cozily together on the couch.

Elizabeth was captivated by the film from the first scene. And when Gary Cooper kissed Grace Kelly, stiff and closed mouthed as suited the mores of the era, all she could think about was that she wouldn't want Finn to kiss her that way. He seemed as into the film as she was. Arm around her, he had leaned back against the sofa, watching intently. Occasionally he would stroke her back and legs or lean down to kiss her on the forehead. But he hadn't made a move.

At eleven twenty-five and again at eleven-forty his hand found itself somewhere she didn't want it, and she moved slightly both times as if she were simply repositioning herself for comfort. At least, that's how she hoped she came across.

She riveted her attention to the screen as Will and Amy rode off together on their wedding day and the movie ended. Elizabeth wiped her tears on Finn's arm, and he smiled as he got up to turn off the television. "You're a romantic," he told her, sitting back down next to her.

The room was dark and quiet. He grasped her chin in his fingers and started to kiss her. Deeper, faster, harder. He pressed her against the back of the sofa, his hands in her hair, then on her shoulders, then slipping off the shoulder of the dress.

Panic. All Elizabeth felt was panic.

"Finn, stop," she whispered.

She heard him sigh as he pulled away from her. *Tell him,* she ordered herself. *Just tell him, and he'll understand. It'll solve all your problems.*

"Finn, there's something you need to know." Holding on to Finn's hands, she crossed her legs and faced him.

33

"You can tell me anything, Liz," Finn said. "You know that."

She took a deep breath and looked him right in the eyes. "I'm a virgin."

Finn stared at her for a second, then gave her the biggest, sweetest smile she had ever seen in her life. "Oh, Elizabeth," he said. "Why didn't you tell me before?"

Elizabeth felt herself blush. "I don't know. I guess I felt sort of embarrassed, maybe. Like you'd think I was a kid or something."

Finn's beautiful smile beamed back at her even more brightly. "I'd never think that. And you don't have to say anything more. We can go as slow as you want."

She felt an enormous wave of relief wash her from head to toe. Why was she so scared of everything? "Oh, Finn, I'm so glad you understand. I'm just—I'm just scared. Of how I feel about you, about making love for the first time—"

Finn took her in his arms sweetly and held her. "Shhh," he cooed. "No need to worry about anything more. I'm going to take good care of you. Nice and slow, okay?"

Again they lay together on the couch, and again their kisses grew more earnest as they migrated from lips to face to neck to ears and back. Elizabeth felt completely safe, and she relaxed. They were only making out, and she knew that this time, Finn wouldn't progress it beyond that. He understood now, and he'd promised her he'd take it slow.

But his hand had found the zipper on her dress, and he was inching it down. Elizabeth stiffened. "Finn, I thought—"

"Elizabeth," he said, nuzzling her neck, "we're in love, we're exclusive. . . . I don't understand what's wrong."

"But you said we could take it slow!" she protested.

"But I thought that was what we were doing," he said, looking at her now. "Taking it slow. We don't have to move into the bedroom right away. We can stay right here for a little while, and then—"

Omigod. He didn't understand what she'd been trying to say, and she hadn't understood what he'd meant. She sucked in a deep breath, unsure what to say exactly. Why was this so difficult?

"Um, Finn, I meant take it slow, like, between us. I mean, I'm not ready yet. I'm scared. I thought you understood that."

"I thought I did too, Liz. I thought you understood how I felt too, how I feel about you. Don't you trust me?"

Elizabeth looked at him, her heart in her throat. She could feel the little pinpricks of tears welling up in her eyes. "I d-do trust you," she choked out. "I'm just not ready yet to go all the way!"

"*Go all the way?*" Finn asked with a dry laugh. "Oh God, Liz, that is so high school. I can't believe you said that."

The tears threatened to overflow, and she didn't want him to see her cry. Talk about high school. "I—I—I—" She got up and zipped up her dress to the neck. "I think I should go home, okay?"

He looked at her, his expression full of concern. He finally nodded, then silently grabbed his car keys.

Finn said very little, as did Elizabeth, during the drive to her duplex. Through the windshield she stared up at the indifferent stars, grateful that she'd conquered her tears.

Finn reached over and gave her hand a little squeeze. She smiled weakly, and he smiled back thoughtfully. So maybe things weren't ruined between them, she said to herself, gnawing on her lower lip. Maybe this wasn't the end?

When they reached her house, he walked her to the door, and she turned her face up to his for a kiss good night. But Finn only smiled, squeezed her elbow, and gave her a peck on the cheek.

"I'll call you," he said, then turned and walked back to his car.

*   *   *

Sam barely maintained control of his roaring red Indy racer as he rounded the final corner of the track and shot across the finish line—just ahead of the other cars. He eased his grip on the Playstation controller and glanced over at Bugsy. Bugsy realized he had just lost the race and let out a pained sigh, slumping back against the couch as his joystick dropped to the floor between his feet.

"And as the champion repeats his victory," Sam announced, in the hushed voice of a television sportscaster, "an eerie silence descends upon the crowd at Indianapolis."

"Speaking of eerie silence," Bugsy began, reaching down to pick up his controller, "where is everybody? On a Monday night I thought your housemates would all be home, making cupcakes for an SVU bake sale or something."

"Maybe Elizabeth," Sam answered. "But Jessica wouldn't even know how to turn on an oven, and I'm eternally grateful that Neil Martin is a good cook. They're all out somewhere."

Sam wished that Elizabeth *was* in the kitchen, making cupcakes or eating one of her endless cups of yogurt. Anywhere but out with that jerk Finn. Or worse, *in* with that jerk Finn. In his apartment. In his bedroom . . .

He heard a key twisting in the front door and turned around, surprised to see Elizabeth enter the house. Her shoulders were slumped forward, and her head was slightly bowed. She was clearly very upset. When she looked up to see Sam staring at her, she quickly turned her head and made a beeline for the stairs.

But not before Sam had noticed she was crying. Damn.

"Bugs, I'll be back in a little while," he told his friend. "I need to go ask Wakefield something."

Bugsy nodded and turned his attention back to the game. Sam headed for the stairs.

I guess Wakefield confronted Dr. Cool tonight about what I told her, he realized. *And the mack daddy of med school must have fessed up.*

Chapter
Four

Elizabeth pulled on her thick, terry-cloth robe and tied it around her, then flopped down on her bed and burst into tears.

No kiss good night. No "it's okay." No "I love you."

Just an "I'll call you."

Because she *was* "so high school." Finn was absolutely right.

Why didn't she feel ready? What was wrong with her?

She thought about the girls she always saw around campus, kissing their boyfriends on the lawns. She wondered how many of those couples were having sex. She knew that Jessica wasn't a virgin. And her best friend, Nina Harper, wasn't a virgin either. They'd also both been very much in love for their first times, Elizabeth knew.

But they'd both been very sure that they were ready. The relationships might not have lasted in either case, but Elizabeth knew that neither girl regretted losing their virginity to those particular guys. It had been right at the time.

So why doesn't this feel totally right to me? Elizabeth wondered for the millionth time. *If I'm in love, and Finn's in love with me, and we're an exclusive couple now . . . what's my problem?*

She heard three soft taps on the door. Jessica! Elizabeth thought. Just the person she needed to talk to.

"Jess?" she called out hopefully, springing up from her bed.

"No, it's me, Sam."

Elizabeth's heart sank, and she dropped back down on the bed. He was exactly the opposite of what she needed right now.

"Wakefield?" The door opened a little, and he poked his head through.

"G-Go away," she said with a sniffle.

Sam came in anyway and leaned against the wall by her vanity table. "So he confessed, huh?"

Elizabeth groped to follow his meaning. What was he talking about? "Confessed to what?" she snapped.

He sighed. "About being in Frankie's with that girl."

Was he still on this stupid lie? "You made it up,

Sam. Why would I even ask him about it?"

"*Whatever*, Wakefield," he said. "From the looks of you, I can only guess that your night didn't go too well. And I can't say I'm sorry for that. The guy's cheating on you—I saw it with my own eyes. *He's* not the virgin, *he's* not the one who could get pregnant, and mark my words, he's probably out at Starlights right now, flirting with some other girl. He's not the one home crying. He's out there trying to get some."

Elizabeth glared at him, unable to believe his nerve. She was caught between screaming at him to mind his own business, telling him he was an idiot, punching him in the stomach, and physically throwing him out of her room. How dare he lecture her on anything!

"You have one second to get out of here, Sam," she said between clenched teeth.

"I'm gonna say this for the last time, Wakefield. You can do what you want—it's your body, and it's your broken heart. But I saw him pawing some girl. He's just trying to get in your pants. You're nothing more than a conquest to him. That might sound harsh, but so's the reality of getting dumped after you give it up."

"Sam," she screamed. "Shut up. Shut, shut, shut, shut up! I think you're forgetting that not all guys are like *you*. That's who you're talking about here. You. *You're* the kind of guy who'd do something like that. Finn isn't. So just get out of here!"

"I'm not lying, Liz," he said. Those intense hazel eyes stared at her. But he had no expression on his face. He didn't look like he was having fun, he didn't look upset, he didn't look bored—he didn't look *anything*.

Sam Burgess, who couldn't handle a real conversation, was spending a little too long on this, she realized. She had no idea why, and she really didn't care.

It's a game to him, she suddenly understood. Just like everything else in his life. She sprang off her bed and grabbed him by the front of his shirt, twisting it in her fist. "Listen to me," she stated inches from his face. "You know nothing about Finn. Your story is an out-and-out lie. I do not believe a single word you say about him. Mind your own business!"

He raised his eyebrow at her, and she let go of him, then walked back to her bed and sat down in as dignified a manner as she could.

"I'll be the first to say I told you so, Wakefield." He turned to go, smug as could be.

She picked up one of her Beanie Babies from her nightstand and fired it at Sam's back. He paused, then disappeared out the door.

A seed of fatigue glowed in the pit of her misery like an ember. Elizabeth laid her face on her soft pillow and felt the tears spill once more. She lay still, nursing the ember of fatigue into a flame of sleepiness. Eventually she was able to cry herself to sleep.

Xavier handed Nina another glass of red wine, and she smiled and took a sip. She couldn't believe she, Nina Harper, had been hanging out backstage for hours with the band and their girlfriends. Her life was taking such amazing twists and turns!

When Francesca had introduced them, Nina had nervously extended her hand as if to a potential employer at a job interview. Xavier had shaken her hand, holding it for an extra second and looking her steadily in the eyes.

"So, now that we've been hanging out for a while," Xavier said, sipping his own drink, "I've gotta come clean. I was *dying* to meet you."

"Me too," she gushed.

Xavier smiled. "I saw you in the audience, and I couldn't keep my eyes off you, especially when you moved up close to the stage. In fact, I almost forgot my words a couple of times."

Nina could feel herself blushing. She barely believed her ears. "You could really see me? I mean, I could see you. Duh, of course, you were up on the stage, singing. But I just thought that with all those lights shining and flashing in your face and everything that maybe you couldn't really see me down there. That maybe I was just imagining it."

"You weren't imagining it, Nina," Xavier insisted. "And I know this is going to sound corny, but I really felt like we made a connection tonight. I mean, as much as two people can without talking. Or touching. But the way you move to the music, it's like you understand what we're doing."

"Oh, please," Nina protested. "I'm like the world's worst dancer. My friends always tease me that I dance like Elaine on *Seinfeld*."

Xavier gave her a look that said he didn't get the reference. "So what's your favorite Wired song?" he asked.

"I don't know the name of it," she told him, "but it's the one that goes, 'I wanna be super. I wanna be your superhero.'"

Xavier looked pleased. "Wow, you were really paying attention, huh?"

"How couldn't I?" Nina beamed. "You guys are *so* good. I can't wait to hear you play again."

Xavier shuffled his feet slightly. Was he uncomfortable with all of Nina's enthusiastic attention? She silently cautioned herself not to be so eager. "To tell you the truth," Nina added, "I almost never go to see live music."

"So, you're more into raves and techno or what? Where do you usually go out?" Xavier didn't seem to be just making conversation. He seemed to really want to know the answers to his questions.

"Actually, I hardly ever go out at night," Nina answered reluctantly. "Unless it's to the library."

Great! she thought. *Now he knows I'm a big dweeb. The library? Why did I just admit that I spend my nights at the library? Why couldn't I have just made something up?* Nina braced herself for the inevitable diss.

"Oh, so you're a scholar, eh?" Xavier put a thoughtful hand on his chin and looked Nina up and down, as if appraising her in a whole new light. "A beautiful scholar. Hmmm. So, what's your major?"

"Physics," she said, bracing herself.

"Wow," Xavier commented. "You are a scholar! My dad's a biochemist. He works in a research lab."

Nina's interest was piqued. "Really? So do I. It's my work-study job on campus."

The conversation drifted from talk of their parents, to what it was like growing up on opposite sides of the country, and on to Xavier's theories about the right and left sides of the brain. As the night went on, Nina felt closer and closer to him.

She forgot all about Francesca, and Xavier seemed equally oblivious to his band mates. After what seemed like hours of talking, Nina found herself happily sharing a ratty green couch in the corner of the room with Xavier. She couldn't believe how different he was from the person she imagined while watching him perform.

There was no big rock-star ego. In fact, he was surprisingly humble and self-aware. And not just creative, but incredibly intelligent. And he seemed so interested in learning more about Nina. She only wished she had a more interesting life to share with him. As all of Xavier's desirable qualities were running through Nina's mind, he leaned in close to whisper a question.

"Nina, I've been wanting to ask you this ever since we sat down together." She could feel his sweet, hot breath tickling her ear. "Can I kiss you?"

Nina answered without words, moving her mouth to meet his supple lips. Xavier let Nina set the pace. It started with a series of soft touches between the lips. But soon their kisses were deeper than even the heartfelt conversation they had shared. Nina had never been one for public displays of affection, but then again, she had never met anyone quite like Xavier before.

As she ran her hands across the firm contours of his chest, she was no longer conscious of the other people talking and milling about the room. She was totally in the moment, savoring each touch, each kiss, each caress.

When she finally came to her senses, Nina

realized that she and Xavier were the only two people remaining in the room. "Where is everyone?" she wondered out loud.

Xavier seemed reluctant to emerge from their intimate bliss. His voice was slow and tired. "I don't know. But all our stuff is still here, so the guys must be around somewhere. They're probably getting drinks at the bar."

As if on cue, Billy poked his head through the door. "The bar's closed, man. Come on—we gotta start getting this equipment together."

"All right." Xavier hesitated. "I'll be right there, okay?" He looked at Nina on the green couch beside him. "I guess I have to go. But hey, I really want to see you again."

"Me too." Nina gave an easy smile.

"I mean, I'd like to walk you home. But I guess I better help the guys with the equipment and everything."

"That's okay!" Nina was way too blissed out to care. Besides, she wouldn't have expected him to walk her home anyway. "I don't live far away at all—right on campus."

"Cool." Xavier planted one last quick, sweet kiss on Nina's ready lips.

"But just a minute." Nina grabbed her purse and fished around for a pen. She scribbled her number on a scrap of paper and handed it to Xavier. She couldn't remember the last time she had voluntarily given her digits to a guy. But this was no ordinary guy. "Why don't you call me sometime?"

Xavier took the paper and casually slipped it into his back pocket. "I'll definitely call you."

Nina was walking on clouds as she emerged from the club into the warm night air. Francesca had left her behind, but Nina didn't even care. She had been so caught up in Xavier's kisses, who could blame her? She glanced at her watch for the first time since going backstage. Almost 3 A.M.! But tonight was well worth risking a C on that calc test.

Sam rolled over on his side for what felt like the fiftieth time. He looked again at the glowing green digits of his alarm clock. 3:06 A.M.

He had already counted hundreds of sheep, named every one of his teachers from kindergarten through twelfth grade, and run through the alphabet twice, first thinking of cities that began with each letter and then moving on to Sweet Valley street names. And his eyelids still didn't feel any heavier. *I guess I'll revert to the opium of the masses,* he decided. *Television.*

Sam rose wearily from his bed, pulled on a pair of soft old Levi's, and made his way to the living room. He grabbed the remote and flicked on the tube. The familiar face of Sally Struthers was somehow reassuring as she spoke out about starving children in Africa. He cruised past infomercials for *Songs of the Seventies,* the amazing Fat Assassin, and How to Get Rich by Investing in Yourself. He lingered on an old episode of *CHiPs* just long enough to see the climactic car crash and finally settled on a rerun of that day's *Jerry Springer.*

Terrence, the ugliest dude Sam had ever seen, was surrounded by four women who Sam could only imagine encountering in a jail cell. Terrence was secretly seeing all of them and wanted to come clean on national television.

Sam shook his head in disbelief. *How could those women be so stupid?* he wondered. *Or actually be attracted to that loser?* He was reminded of Dr. Cool, with his stable of unwitting undergrads.

Once again Sam caught himself dwelling on Elizabeth's situation with Finn. Why did he care so much about what was going on with them? Was it just because he now had proof that Finn was cheating on her? That every smooth word that came out of his mouth was a total lie?

Sam was well aware he had deep and mysterious feelings for Elizabeth. Feelings he had no interest in digging into or exploring or acknowledging. She was able to see inside him in a way no other girl could. Which was the problem, of course. There were reasons Sam hid behind his sarcastic slacker exterior.

Never in a million years would Sam go down the Elizabeth road again. But the feelings were there, period, and there was nothing he could do about them—except ignore them as best he could and keep a brick wall between himself and Elizabeth.

Still, there was no way he'd sit by and let Elizabeth get used by some sleaze.

He turned his attention back to the television, trying to tune out thoughts of Elizabeth with Dr. Cool. The show was giving him an idea. All he had to do was show her what guys like Finn were really like. What players did to girls. And since Elizabeth thought *he* was the biggest player around, Sam was the perfect guy to play this little role.

Chapter
Five

Todd Wilkins handed his battered copy of his add/drop form to the woman behind the counter at the bursar's office. "Someone left me a message saying I had to come in and bring my form— something about it not getting stamped properly," Todd explained.

As the woman looked at his form and then clicked away at the keyboard of her computer, Todd wondered what had possessed him to sign up for all those courses in the first place. Biology, art history, and intro to philosophy? What had he been thinking?

He'd bombed his first biology test. Exploring his aptitude for science was one experiment that was destined to blow up in his face.

Art history was an equally dismal failure. The windowless room with no ventilation or air-conditioning, combined with the monotonous drone of a failed sculptor masquerading as a professor, made it impossible for Todd to stay awake when the lights went off and the slide projector went on.

And intro to philosophy was a similarly effective sedative. Even when he thought he understood what the professor had said in the lecture, he could never think of anything relevant to add in his discussion section. And somehow the word "Huh?" didn't seem to fit into the philosophical discourse.

Besides, it wasn't like any of those classes had any relevance to real life. He certainly wasn't going to go into medicine, he already knew enough about art to know what he liked when he saw it in a museum (the one time he went to a museum anyway), and the only burning question he had about life was, "What am I going to do with mine?"

So he was glad he'd decided to ease his load considerably. Not only could he stop worrying about messing up in classes he had no use for, but he'd have more time to work at Frankie's. He'd spoken to his boss, Rita, about taking on more shifts, and she'd green-lighted him. That meant more money.

Since he was living off campus and paying for everything himself, he had plenty of important things to spend his new and improved paycheck on. Like rent and food. And eventually a Harley-Davidson. He couldn't wait until he'd saved up enough to buy a bike and give his parents back the BMW. A real adult who had his own apartment and a job and part-time schoolwork didn't drive around in his daddy's luxury car.

"Okay, Mr. Wilkins," the woman behind the counter said. "The problem was that our records indicated your form wasn't stamped No Refund when you turned it in. And it has to be for our records. You *were* informed that you'd missed the deadline for receiving a partial refund for dropped classes, correct?"

"Uh, yeah, I think so," Todd told her. "Whatever."

She stared at him. "You don't care that you're not entitled to get any money back for those three classes?"

"Oh, well, that's my parents' money," Todd explained. "It comes right out of a bank account they set up for me. It's not like *I* paid for the classes."

The woman was glaring at him. Todd realized how he'd just sounded. "No, you don't understand," he rushed to add. "I never use that account for anything but tuition and books. I haven't dipped into it once since moving off campus. I'm paying for everything other than school myself. I'm not mooching off my parents like all the other kids at this school."

She snorted. "But you're willing to *throw away* their money by having dropped these classes after the deadline for even a partial refund. No medal there, kid."

The woman stamped his form No Refund and handed it back to him. "Your parents won't receive notice of these dropped classes," she added. "They only would if they were to receive a refund. At least they won't know that you've wasted thousands of their dollars."

Was this clerk allowed to talk to him that way? Todd wondered. Here he was, trying to live like an adult and pay his own way, for his own rent, food, fun, and anything else, and this woman was treating him like the worst moocher at SVU.

He stuffed the form in his back pocket and headed outside. The minute he felt the sunshine on his shoulders he realized that the nasty clerk had actually made his day. He *hadn't* known that his parents wouldn't be informed that he'd dropped classes. And it didn't take a scientist or a philosopher to know what they would have thought about that!

Since he hadn't discussed the decision to cut his schedule in half with his parents in the first place, Todd knew that they'd be none too happy to receive a mysterious refund check in the mail.

Remember what you're doing here, Todd, he reminded himself. *The whole reason you're upping your hours at Frankie's is to earn money on your own. To be independent. To not have to rely on Mom and Dad for anything. And to not have to answer to them for every single decision you make about what you do with your time.*

Besides, Todd told himself, *now Mom and Dad won't know a thing about my new part-time schedule until* next *semester, when the tuition bill is suddenly cut in half!*

Todd was sure that by that time, he'd have a much easier time convincing his folks how much he needed to be more self-sufficient. And he'd be able to show them how much better his life was now that he was practically supporting himself. Still, he wasn't exactly looking forward to *that* conversation. But he *was* looking forward to all the great money he'd be making at Frankie's.

Chloe stood on line in the cafeteria, wishing the hulking frat guy in front of her would make up his mind already. She had her eye on the tuna sandwich and the fat-free devil's-food cake.

Giggle. Giggle-giggle. Chloe turned around and saw her two biggest nightmares grab trays and plunk them down next to hers. Whisper. Giggle. Whisper-whisper.

Lindsay and Johanna, two seniors from Theta's "old guard," were the least friendly sisters Chloe had met during all the rush parties.

She remained facing forward and hoped they wouldn't notice her. But of course that was impossible. Chloe had never been a lucky person.

Her stomach was in knots. She bit her bottom lip from a combination of nervousness and extreme dread. It was pledge week. And for a Theta pledge that meant only one thing: humiliation. Chloe knew the rules, and she knew that Theta sisters like Johanna and Lindsay would show her no mercy.

She continued to look straight ahead and prepared herself as best she could to be degraded in front of everyone else within fifty feet of her. She didn't have to wait long. She felt Johanna's icy breath on the back of her neck as her future sister whispered urgently in her ear, "Listen, Chloe, you're about to have your first test as a Theta pledge."

Chloe turned her head slightly to look at her tormentor, but Johanna stopped her. "Do *not* look at me," Johanna hissed. "Just do exactly as I say, and don't *you* say anything."

Chloe nodded nervously. She knew what was coming. Her heart raced with a mix of anxiety and exhilaration. She wasn't looking forward to making a fool of herself in the cafeteria, but she knew she had to do it if she wanted to fulfill her dream of becoming a Theta. And that's precisely what she wanted. Desperately.

"Okay," Johanna continued in an authoritative whisper. "See that guy in front of you? The big football player with the Britney Spears look-alike by his side?"

Chloe nodded once.

"All right. His name is Mike Simmons, and he's a Sigma senior," she explained.

"Now, I think you know about a certain pledge requirement involving guys from Sigma," Lindsay added with a hiss.

Again Chloe nodded, still facing straight ahead.

"Okay, I want you to tap him lightly on the left shoulder with your left hand." Johanna's explicit instructions were completely unnecessary, but the Theta sister was obviously enjoying her role as drill sergeant. "When he turns around to face you, grab his neck with both hands and give him the biggest kiss of his life. On the lips, of course. Open mouth. Of course."

Chloe nodded nervously once more.

Lindsay whispered one last urgent instruction. "And you can't say anything to him—you just have to do it."

Chloe braced herself to make a scene. She quickly glanced around the room to see if there was anyone she knew. At a nearby table was Val's dowdy roommate, Deena, tucking into a cheeseburger. For a split second Chloe envied the antisocial loner in sweatpants and faded T-shirt.

All Deena had to worry about was her classes, while Chloe was about to make a foolish spectacle of herself in the middle of SVU's main cafeteria. But the envy gave way to fleeting pity as Chloe reminded herself why she was willing to go through with this stunt. While Deena was no doubt headed for a life of friendlessness, Chloe was on track to actually being someone on the SVU campus. Soon she would be a Theta, and all the nervousness, dread, and humiliation of pledge week would be behind her.

Chloe took a deep breath, exhaled, and tapped Mike on the left shoulder. As he turned around to see who it was, Chloe reached up and clasped her hands around the back of his neck. His jaw dropped in surprise, and Chloe swiftly pulled his gaping mouth toward hers. Her lips made a dramatic smack, and she practically shoved her tongue down his throat before he could pull away in horror.

Unfortunately for both of them, her grip was too tight, and he couldn't break free. It was up to his girlfriend, Lauren, to break them apart. The Britney Spears look-alike let out a shriek and grabbed Chloe by the hair. With her other hand she pushed Mike's chest back and then used both hands to violently shove Chloe backward into the cackling Theta sisters behind her. Chloe nearly lost her balance from the force of the push, but

Johanna and Lindsay held her up and forced her back toward Mike and his livid girlfriend. "You little slut!" the Britney girlfriend shouted. "What do you think you're doing?"

Somehow Chloe felt like she was watching from a vantage point high above the cafeteria, seeing the entire scene unfolding in slow motion below her. She even saw Deena put down her burger to shake her head in disapproving disbelief.

"I had to . . ." Chloe listened to her disembodied voice as if there were cotton in her ears.

And then she was back again, looking helplessly at the girlfriend, who seemed about to scratch out Chloe's eyes and toss them across the room. Chloe looked wide-eyed at the irate girl and pointed to the pledge pin on her own sweater. "I'm a pledge, a pledge. . . ."

The words sounded ridiculous coming out of her mouth, and somehow the laughter that filled the room kept getting louder and louder. She looked imploringly at Johanna and Lindsay, who stared at her in hysterics, practically falling over themselves in maniacal amusement.

Chloe was so flustered and ashamed that she couldn't bear to be in the room another second. She mumbled something about being late for class, had to run. And that's exactly what she did. Full speed she fled from the uproar of the caf, the overwhelming laughter ringing in her ears until she finally made it outside.

At last Chloe could catch her breath and try to calm herself. She had passed her first test of pledge week. She should have felt great, thankful to Lindsay and Johanna for the chance to prove herself. But instead she felt violated and abused.

Her new feelings toward Johanna and Lindsay weren't at all like sisterly love. No, they were more like the sentiments one reserved for enemies. And that's exactly what Johanna and Lindsay were to her now. Chloe looked back toward the cafeteria and imagined Johanna and Lindsay's laughing faces. She swore to herself that one day she'd get them back—once she became a full-fledged Theta.

Todd walked across campus, trying to put the whole bursar's-office debacle behind him. He felt a twinge of guilt over wasting his parents' money on credits that would no longer count toward graduation. If he ever even graduated. He wondered if it might be best to take the next semester off entirely. But deep down, he knew his parents would never go for that. They'd have a hard enough time accepting his new part-time schedule.

"Todd, what's up?"

He glanced up to see Neil Martin walking

toward him with his signature grin pleasantly plastered to his face.

"Oh, hey, Neil." Todd caught himself sounding less than enthusiastic as he greeted his friend for the first time since the summer. The two of them had spent weeks together in a motor home as teammates in a cross-country contest, but they had never managed to grow very close. Neil spent most of his time palling around with Jessica Wakefield, and Todd was usually preoccupied with overcoming the urge to strangle another teammate, Tom Watts—the very guy who'd ended up sleeping with his girlfriend, Dana.

Ex-girlfriend, Todd corrected himself. Sometimes it was still weird to think that he and Dana had been living together just a short time ago.

"Man, I haven't seen you all semester." Neil reached out to shake Todd's hand. "Where have you been keeping yourself?"

"Oh, I live off campus now, and I'm only going to school part-time." It felt good to say that, Todd had to admit, since he thought it set him apart from most of the other students at SVU.

"Cool." Neil nodded. "I'm living off campus too. Sharing a house with Jessica and Elizabeth and Sam Burgess. You remember Sam from the contest, right?"

"Uh-huh." Todd hoped he didn't sound too bitter as he thought back to the summer static between him and Sam over Elizabeth. "I actually ran into Burgess the other night. So, what have you been up to, Neil?"

"Oh, you know, mostly just school stuff. Taking a pretty heavy load of classes. And I ran for student-body president, but I lost." Neil shrugged.

"That sucks, man." Todd tried to sound sincere even though student-body president was probably the last thing on his list of worthwhile activities.

"Yeah, well, it was probably for the best." Neil forced a smile. Then his tone brightened as he changed the subject. "Todd, hey—we just decided this morning to have this party Saturday night at the house. You know, Jessica and Elizabeth and me. We're all sort of hosting it. Oh, and Sam too, I guess. But I think it's going to be mostly SVU people. You should stop by."

At Neil's invitation to the party, a flurry of thoughts instantly passed through Todd's head. He certainly wasn't interested in seeing Sam again. Once every three months was more than enough. Though he did have to admit that Sam had acted pretty cool the other night when he had run into him. And he couldn't be all bad if he hung out at Frankie's. No one from SVU ever went to Frankie's. But then again, Sam went to OCC, not SVU. Todd guessed that was another reason not to hate him.

But Jessica was another story. After all the crap she'd pulled and all the headaches she'd caused

Todd and the team during the contest last summer, she was the last person he wanted to party with. And then there was Elizabeth. He couldn't help but feel a faint longing for his ex-girlfriend, even though it had been a year since their breakup.

But then he imagined Elizabeth asking him about Dana and school and all the other things she thought were important to him. Things that in reality he was completely over. No, he didn't have much interest in hanging with the Wakefield twins.

Thinking about Neil's housemates, Todd was glad that now he was friends with so many non-SVU people. One more reason to be thankful for his job at Frankie's. But still, Todd reminded himself, a party's a party: free drinks, munchies, and, knowing the Wakefields, plenty of cute girls. Even if they would be mostly SVUers.

But just because that SVU chick he had taken out the week before was totally superficial and completely wrapped up in her own little artificial college existence (not to mention that she had totally dissed him for the direction *his* life was taking) didn't mean that every single girl at Sweet Valley University had to be the same way.

Todd looked back at Neil, who was still waiting for an answer to his invitation. "Sure, Neil, that sounds great." He tried to sound excited about the party. "I'll definitely stop by."

Chapter Six

Elizabeth sat alone on a ledge alongside the floor-to-ceiling windows that made up the front wall of the mezzanine level of the SVU student center. From her perch she could see almost halfway across the quadrangle plaza. Hundreds of brightly clad young people milled and swirled in the space below her. The variety was amazing, she thought. She knew a lot of people at SVU, but the school was so big that she could sit here for an hour without seeing a single familiar face. *So many faces, so many stories,* she reflected.

How many of them are wondering if they're ready for sex? she asked herself, scanning every face as it passed beneath her for some clue. Her view was perfect, and the bright autumn light flecked the sea of faces like whitecaps on waves.

Finn! There he was. She saw him instantly, still

rather far away, his golden head above the surface of the crowd like the sun, smoothly navigating through the current of bodies in his familiar, graceful, long-limbed way.

Elizabeth stood up and pressed herself against the window. She was dying to rush downstairs, to give him a kiss hello, to tell him she missed him already, which was true. *But you can't do that,* she told herself. *You can't run after him like that. Not after last night.*

She stepped back from the window. *He'll call,* she reminded herself. *We'll go out; we'll talk.* Elizabeth stamped her foot a little and clutched her arms to her stomach. *Why are you making such a big deal out of this?* she wondered. *You see your boyfriend on the quad, you go up to him. "I saw you from the mezz in the student center, Finn. Wanna grab lunch?"*

Don't do it, Lizzie, she ordered herself. *Don't chase him.*

Finn's golden head was getting closer to the entrance beneath her window seat. He looked perfect, of course, in his tailored camel's-hair blazer, faded jeans, and old loafers. Maybe she should just say hi. She could just pretend to bump into him, of course. But then what would she do? Would they go and talk? Have coffee? So that would be another "date"?

No, we're "exclusive" now, Elizabeth reminded

herself. They were "going out." When you were "going out," you didn't "count dates." Suddenly the vocabulary seemed stupid and senseless to her. *Oh God, Liz, that's so high school. . . .*

He reached inside his jacket pocket, withdrew his sunglasses, and put them on, and Elizabeth forced away his words. They'd been said in frustration. Nothing more. He hadn't meant to be mean.

She watched him walk toward the library. She was glad he'd moved on; now she *couldn't* rush downstairs and pretend to bump into him. She relaxed her stance and absorbed his profile from head to toe. He wore no socks, and she could see his ankle peeking out above his beat-up brown leather loafers. His soccer-player's thighs filled his worn blue jeans firmly, from his taut white canvas belt to his knees, where the denim was worn almost entirely away. An oversized white oxford shirt ballooned up from under his elbow-patched blazer in the breeze.

God, he was gorgeous.

He seemed to be thinking very hard about something. He tapped his fingers on his chin. Then he stood next to the wall for a moment, fished a little notebook out of his back pocket, extracted a pencil stub from it, and began to write a few words.

The whole plaza was growing more crowded

and lively before Elizabeth's eyes. The double doors of the main classroom building opened wide, and a flood of student bodies inundated the whole quarter. She lost sight of Finn in the rush, then she spotted him again. He'd been joined by a redhead in a blue sweater. *Don't you have anywhere to go?* Elizabeth thought crossly as she eyed the pretty girl.

Elizabeth watched stonily as the girl did most of the talking. Finn laughed a couple of times, but she could tell he wasn't the one keeping the conversation going. *Get going, redhead. Lunchtime's over. Back to class.*

But they just stood there. Finally the girl said something, twisting her hands. The girl persisted after something, gesturing at Finn's notebook.

What did she want? Elizabeth wondered nervously. The girl pointed to the page, then said something else. Finn wrote down what she was saying. *I knew it!* Elizabeth thought stormily. *She's giving him her phone number! Aargh!*

Elizabeth watched the girl walk away. Finn settled himself back against the wall by the concrete bench. He looked down at his little notebook without emotion. He seemed to be lost in thought. He *didn't ask for her number,* Elizabeth thought. She was sure of it. The girl had simply offered it.

Elizabeth ripped the scrunchie from her hair

and shook out her ponytail, then pulled off her sweatshirt and smoothed down the cropped white baby tee she wore underneath. Throwing her knapsack over her shoulder, Elizabeth flew down the stairs. She had to catch him. Or some other girl would.

Sam sat on an orange-and-brown modular chair in the drab, cinder-block student center of Orange County College. He had only been on the SVU campus a couple of times, but he knew for certain that it was a lot more styling than the broken-down 1970s architecture and interiors of OCC. But what did Sam need with fancy buildings, fine oak furniture, and manicured lawns? He had enough of that where he came from.

And Boston, thankfully, was three thousand miles away.

Besides, he was perfectly comfortable with the low-profile setting of his college of choice. The girls at this school were just as cute as any he had seen at SVU. And most of them were a lot less stuck-up. Proof of that was right in front of him.

Anna Wilcox, without question the most beautiful sophomore in his twentieth-century fiction course, squinted at Sam in an effort to understand. "So, let me make sure I've got this straight. You want to make your housemate realize her boyfriend's a creep by acting like one yourself."

"Exactly," Sam told her. He and Anna had dated for a while last year, but they'd quickly discovered they had more chemistry as friends, and they'd been buds ever since. She was perfect for the role of his supposed "sexual conquest."

Anna placed her palms on the table between them. "So, the two of you are housemates—friends, but nothing more. You like her, but you don't *like* like her. You *fooled around* over the summer, but you were never actually *going out*. But you do want to steal her away from this new boyfriend. Now, do I have it right so far?"

"Everything except for that last part—I'm not trying to *steal her away* from anyone," Sam insisted. "I just want to get her away from the creep."

"Because if you can't have her, then no one can, right?"

"Wrong." Sam groaned. "That's not what this is about, Anna. I don't want her. I just want to wake her up to what this Finn guy is all about."

"And what, exactly, is that?"

Anna's penchant for challenging nearly everything he said happened to be one of his favorite qualities in her. It was the same reason why he liked Elizabeth so much. But he'd never really been attracted to Anna, and he had been attracted to Elizabeth. *Was* attracted, maybe. Which was why he could deal with being friends with Anna and not with Elizabeth.

Still, Anna's challenging ways weren't exactly making this conversation easy. "Well, of course I don't know what he's *all* about, but I knew from the minute they met that he was a jerk, and now I have proof he's cheating on her. And she won't believe me. I just think she needs to find out the real deal—before it's too late."

"Too late?" Anna arched her eyebrows. "Too late for what?"

Too late for what—good question, thought Sam. He didn't really want to share with Anna the deepest secrets of Elizabeth's life, like the fact that she was still a virgin. Or the fact that he'd found this out by overhearing her discussing it with her sister. It was bad enough that he was already butting into Elizabeth's business as much as he was. But of course, it was for her own good.

"B-Before . . . ," Sam stammered. "Before she gets hurt. You know, before she falls into Finn's well-worn bed and then gets kicked to the curb once the conquest is complete."

"Okay, I get it, Sam," Anna began, with more than a hint of sarcasm in her voice. "You want me to pose as one of *your* sexual conquests so you can parade me around in front of Elizabeth the morning after and then kick *me* to the curb until you want another taste. And by

71

doing this, you'll be teaching your housemate what, exactly?"

"It'll teach her what guys like Finn are really like."

"Which is?" Anna raised an eyebrow.

Sam was tempted to throw up his arms and forget the whole thing. "Which is they lie. They cheat. They treat women like disposable razors—they use them up and then throw them away."

"Disposable razors?" Anna laughed at the lame analogy.

"You know what I mean," Sam answered. He was beginning to feel a bit self-conscious. And not just about his use of metaphors. Perhaps he *was* being overly protective.

"You know what I think, Sam? I think you might be overstepping your bounds here as a housemate. I mean, I can appreciate you wanting to save Elizabeth from getting hurt or whatever. But don't you think it might not actually be your place to act?"

Anna's response had echoed his own thoughts, he realized glumly. "Yeah, but—"

"Yeah, but Elizabeth is an adult," Anna interrupted. "She's nineteen. She should be able to take care of herself. And it can't be up to you—or any guy, for that matter—to protect her from getting hurt. I mean, as long as there are men in the world, women are going to get hurt. Simple as that. I'm not saying men are bad and women are wonderful. I'm just saying that where love is concerned, there's always the potential for hurt. Especially if you make the mistake of falling for the wrong person."

Sam nodded in solemn agreement. "Maybe you're right, Anna. But still, I feel like I have to do something." He hesitated. "So, does this mean you're not going to help me?"

Anna reached out and touched Sam's arm reassuringly. "Of course I'll help you, Sam. For one thing, I want to meet this Elizabeth so I can at least see who's getting you so worked up over all of this. Besides, it sounds like it might be fun."

"Really?" Sam had been on the verge of giving up. But now with Anna on board, his plan had a second wind. "So, are you up for it tonight?"

"Tonight, huh?" Anna was suddenly tentative. "Now, tell me again exactly what you have in mind."

"Okay." Sam took a big breath and exhaled. "What I have in mind is this. You come by tonight around nine. We hang out. Rent a movie or whatever. And then whenever Elizabeth gets home, we make it apparent to her that you're spending the night with me. You know, we kiss or whatever and then go into my room together and shut the door."

"And then," Anna said, "we wake up in the morning, you wait till you hear Elizabeth coming downstairs, then you lead me past her to the front door, act all aloof and say you'll call me, then practically throw me out. Is that it?"

Sam nodded. Anna understood this perfectly.

"It's a deal on one condition, Sammy. I get your bed. You get the floor."

"Deal." Sam smiled.

"Finn! Hey!" Elizabeth called in her most I'm-so-surprised-to-see-you-here tone.

He immediately glanced up at the sound of her voice, flashing her a bright smile as he put his little notebook in his jacket pocket. "I was hoping I might run into you," he told her, kissing her on the cheek. "Got time for a walk? I've been standing here for a while working on a chemistry diagram, and if I try to figure it out for one more second, I'll implode."

Elizabeth laughed. "Let's go. *So*, she thought. *The reason he was around the main campus was to look for me!* And she'd been worried about running downstairs when she'd spotted him. *Fool*, she told herself. *That'll teach you to play stupid little games.*

Unless he's here to dump you, she thought nervously.

"We really need to talk, Elizabeth," he began.

Well, here it comes, she realized, bracing herself. *Just don't cry in front of him as he's telling you it's over.*

"I love being with you, Elizabeth. And I meant *everything* I said last night. I am falling in love with you. And I do want it to be just me and you. Nothing that happened—or didn't happen—is going to change that. There's no one else for me but you."

Stunned, Elizabeth stared at him, then jumped into his arms. He laughed and wrapped his arms around her. "Oh, Finn," she whispered, unable to say anything else.

They stood there, holding each other for a few minutes, and Elizabeth had never felt so relieved in her life. He kissed her gently, then took her hand, and they meandered along the brick paths between the lush SVU lawns.

"I do understand your feelings about your virginity, Elizabeth."

She flushed at his explicitness. "Do you?" she asked. "I thought it was different for guys."

"Well, it's just that *any* first time, whether it involves virginity or not, is scary. I'll be nervous for our first time, Elizabeth."

"Really?" she asked, surprised. She couldn't imagine Finn being anything but in total control and confident.

"Really," he told her with a smile. "You're very

special to me. I'm gonna be so nervous that I might not even be able to, um, perform."

He stared down at the path, and she could tell it had cost him to say that. He was being very honest, she thought happily, sharing his intimate concerns. She wasn't the only one who was nervous in this relationship. Why hadn't she realized that? She'd been so self-absorbed!

She didn't quite know how to respond and was relieved when Finn spoke. "You know what I think might help us both? Something called projective anxiety."

"What's that?" she asked.

"When you're faced with doing something that makes you uncomfortable or nervous, all you need to do is *imagine* it going very well, then *visualize* it going well. Eventually you overcome your anxieties."

Projective anxiety. Would that work? she wondered. Was *anxiety* over making love even really the issue? She wasn't sure.

"So, I'm thinking that if we both try projective anxiety," he continued, "we could pick a date and we'll both know that's the day we'll make love for the first time. As it gets closer to the date, we'll have conquered any fears until all we feel is anticipation."

Huh. One minute it was like he was backing off, letting her off the hook, but in the next breath he was pressuring her again.

Projective anxiety. She tried to imagine their bodies, unclothed, pressed together. She tried to imagine him lying on top of her. But her mind balked at the completion of the image. She shivered. Maybe this projective-anxiety stuff didn't work in the first five minutes.

"Why don't we set a date for Saturday?" he suggested as they continued to walk.

Saturday? she thought nervously. This Saturday? Could visualizing work that fast? *I don't know,* she thought. *I can't seem to think straight about this.*

Suddenly she remembered she had a perfect excuse for why Saturday wouldn't work out. "Actually, we've already got plans for Saturday night. My housemates and I are throwing a party, so of course I'm dying to show you off."

"Great!" he said. "We can stay as long as you want. But Saturday will still work out perfectly since you're not going to want to sleep there afterward. The party will go on all night long, it'll be really smoky and gross, and the house will be a mess. You'll be glad to have somewhere else to go."

They'd stopped outside the biochemistry building. Elizabeth gazed into his caramel-colored eyes and tried to think of what to say to him, some way to buy herself a little more time.

Not yet, she thought. Not Saturday. Overnight

at his place? It was just all . . . too much.

Then again, did she really want to wake up in the duplex on Sunday morning and have Sam attack everything Finn said and did the night before at the party? Did she really want to subject herself to his jealous lies about her boyfriend while she was trying to eat breakfast? No way. Now that she thought about it, just because she'd stay overnight at Finn's didn't mean they *had* to make love.

"You're right, Finn," Elizabeth said brightly. "We could probably escape to your place around midnight."

"It's a date, then," he replied. "Saturday night."

Chapter Seven

Sam and Anna leaned back on the daisy-printed sofa in the duplex as George Clooney and Jennifer Lopez shared a passionate kiss on the TV screen. *Out of Sight* was a really good movie, Sam thought, although his ears had been trained more to hear a key twisting in the front door than on the dialogue.

The lights were off, so the television was the only source of illumination in the room. He and Anna were sitting very close together so that they could be ready to act the minute Elizabeth got home.

"See how they're kissing?" Anna said. "Totally believable. Now, that's how it's got to be between you and me when Elizabeth walks in. Completely realistic."

Sam wasn't sure he *could* kiss Anna like George

Clooney was kissing Jennifer Lopez. First off, Sam wasn't that good an actor. To kiss someone with that much intensity and passion, you really had to be into them in a huge way. Second, subtlety could be more useful than hitting Elizabeth over the head. If he and Anna went overboard, Elizabeth might be too sickened by their PDA to even stick around.

He suddenly heard keys jangling in the front door. Anna swung into action. She draped her arms around his shoulders, then planted her lips on his so it would look like they'd been making out heavily for a while.

He heard the door push open. *Get into it, Burgess,* he told himself silently. *You're supposed to be teaching Elizabeth a lesson here. Now, act surprised, and don't forget to get Anna's name wrong.*

At the sound of the door slamming shut, both Sam and Anna bolted upright. Simultaneously they spun their heads to face Elizabeth with perfect looks of embarrassment and surprise.

"Oh, uh, hey, Wakefield. I didn't expect to see you here."

"Why not?" Elizabeth asked. "I do live here, in case you forgot."

"I just thought you'd be out late with Dr. Cool," Sam said. "I was hoping I'd have the house to myself tonight."

Anna jabbed Sam in the ribs with her elbow.

"Oh, yeah. Um, sorry." Sam glanced from Anna to Elizabeth and back to Anna. "Wakefield, this is Erin. Erin, this is one of my housemates, Elizabeth."

"Um, it's *Anna?*" Anna corrected him, in the best duh voice she could muster.

"Oh, right," Sam said, trying to look sheepish. "Sorry about that. The names sound so close, I guess I heard wrong."

"I can't believe you!" Anna murmured playfully, swatting Sam with a pillow on his chest. "Guys!" she added, smiling at Elizabeth.

"Hello, *Anna,*" Elizabeth said.

Anna put on her perkiest voice. "Hi, Elizabeth!" She offered Elizabeth her hand, along with a big, goofy grin. "It's great to meet you. I've heard so much about you from Sam."

Sam gave Anna a subtle elbow in response to her unnecessary improv and cleared his throat. "Well, um, Anna, since the house is kinda crowded now, why don't we take this party into my room? I have this great new CD I've been dying to play for you. In fact, I bought the CD because a song reminded me of you."

He caught Elizabeth rolling her eyes.

"Really?" Anna asked. "That's so sweet! You just totally redeemed yourself for getting my name wrong."

81

"You know," Sam told her, "one of my favorite songs on it is called 'Erin.' I think that's why I got your name confused. I'm really sorry about that."

"That is beyond sweet!" Anna exclaimed, touching the area of her heart. "I'd love to hear it."

Sam smiled at Anna, then shot a devilish grin at Elizabeth. "Well, then, Anna." Sam stood up and held out his hand.

Anna shot up and took his hand. "Isn't Sam the nicest guy, Elizabeth? He must be the easiest person to live with."

Elizabeth stared at Anna as if she'd just beamed down to Earth from planet Idiot. "Oh, yeah, Sam's really nice. Such a thoughtful housemate." He noticed Elizabeth's eyes lingering on the four Dr Pepper cans on the coffee table. Her sodas.

"So, um, have you two been dating long?" Elizabeth directed at Anna while she sorted through the mail.

"Just a couple of weeks now," Anna replied. "We met in lit class at OCC. It's such a cute story how we hooked up. Since I'm on the dean's list, Sam asked if I'd tutor him, but it turns out he was scoring B's in lit the whole time! He was just too shy to ask me out!"

Good move, Anna, Sam thought. He owed her big for that flash of brilliance. Presenting herself as a brain would make Elizabeth realize that Anna *should* be smart enough to see through him.

"It *has* been about two weeks, right, Sam?" Anna asked, beaming a smile at him.

"Exactly thirteen days," Sam responded, bringing Anna's hand to his lips for a gentle kiss. "Thirteen *amazing* days."

Elizabeth's eyebrow shot up. *God, I'm good,* Sam thought.

"Well, let's go, Anna," Sam said. "Elizabeth doesn't need to see this gush fest unfold in her own living room."

"That's Sam for you," Elizabeth said to Anna in her phoniest voice. "Always so considerate!"

He smirked at Elizabeth, then led Anna past her into his bedroom. Elizabeth gave him her patented dirty look before Sam and Anna disappeared into his room.

Well done, he congratulated himself. *Very well done. Elizabeth will be up in her room gnawing at her lower lip for hours.*

Elizabeth yawned, turning the fruit to the top of her breakfast yogurt with a spoon. She stretched on the stool at the kitchen table, then read the same sentence in her journalism textbook for the fourth time. She'd tried to study last night, but she'd been too distracted by thoughts of Finn, Saturday, and that disgusting little scene she'd witnessed in the living room.

Sam's date might be on the dean's list, but the

girl had to be the biggest fool in Sweet Valley if she'd fallen for one word that came out of Sam's mouth.

"I bought the CD because a song reminded me of you. One of my favorite songs on it is called 'Erin.' That's why I got your name confused. . . . Exactly thirteen days . . . "

What a load of bull!

Creak. Creak. Creak-creak-creak. A weird noise was coming from Sam's room beside the kitchen. *Creak!*

What was that? she wondered. Then she heard soft laughter. *Creak, creak, creak-creak. Creeeeeeak.*

Oh. My. God, she thought. *I cannot believe this. That sound is bedsprings bouncing.* Wildly now. Either a rhinoceros was trying to dribble a basketball on Sam's bed, or he was having sex with that girl.

Elizabeth tried to ignore the rhythmic creaking, but it was just too, too *distracting.* She could tell they were trying to be quiet; Anna's laughter was muffled, and Elizabeth could barely make out Sam's occasional voice.

Well, either Sam had suddenly become as considerate and easy to live with as Anna foolishly believed, or he was making sure that whoever got up and was eating breakfast wouldn't necessarily hear him taking advantage of a girl.

At least he had the decency to care about his

own reputation in the house, Elizabeth thought, disgusted by the whole thing.

Suddenly she heard moaning. A girl moaning. The sound of someone in pain. Elizabeth froze on the stool, her hand poised in midair with a spoonful of yogurt.

Does making love hurt that bad? she wondered nervously.

Idiot, she yelled at herself. *You've heard that sound on television and in the movies often enough to know it's not pain causing that moaning.* She shoved the spoon in her mouth. *You have to start getting a very big clue, Elizabeth,* she told herself.

But it is supposed to hurt the first time, isn't it? Elizabeth thought, gnawing on her lip. She'd heard lots of girls say that.

Her thoughts were interrupted by the sound of Sam's door opening with a burst of giggles. Sam and Anna came into the kitchen; Anna was wearing the same pale blue tank minidress she'd had on the night before. Sam wore his rattiest jeans, a wrinkled black T-shirt, and no shoes.

"Oh, hi, Elizabeth," Anna said through an embarrassed giggle. Anna glanced at Sam for some sort of cue, Elizabeth noticed, but Sam was oblivious. Oblivious all of a sudden, she realized.

"Hi," Elizabeth said, pretending to be absorbed by her textbook.

Sam opened a few cabinets by the refrigerator.

85

"Oh, so I guess I don't have any coffee after all," Sam told Anna. "Sorry." Elizabeth saw him glance at his watch. "Man, I can't believe it's so late. I've gotta meet someone in like twenty minutes, so . . ."

Elizabeth saw Anna tilt her head as if she were trying to read him. *What a jerk you are, Sam,* Elizabeth thought. *Not only are you clearly trying to get rid of Anna, but you're also making it clear you've got someone else to see. Maybe even another girl.*

"Oh, so, um, I guess I should get going, then," Anna said tentatively, clearly a little stung. "Is there a bus nearby that'll take me near OCC?"

"Uh, yeah," Sam told her. "You can take the number 42 on the corner of Crescent and Lee, then transfer at Beaumont, and that bus'll drop you at Muggie's coffee shop. That's only like a half-mile walk to campus."

Elizabeth's mouth dropped open.

Sam leaned down and gave Anna a peck on the forehead. "I'll, uh, call, okay?" He sat down at the counter and grabbed the Sweet Valley newspaper.

"Um, okay," Anna said, looking like she was about to cry. "I'll see you soon, then. I had a really great time last night," she added.

"Me too," Sam replied, glancing up at her as he unfolded the sports section. "I'll, uh, see you in class next week."

Anna had been dismissed, and Ms. Dean's List

was clearly smart enough to know that. She gave Elizabeth a little wave with what dignity she had left, then pushed through the kitchen door.

When the front door could be heard closing behind her, Sam got up, reached into a cabinet, and pulled out a full canister of Maxwell House coffee. In stunned silence Elizabeth watched him measure out enough for an entire pot, then pour the water into the coffeemaker.

"I'm hungry enough for an omelet this morning," Sam commented as he pulled open the refrigerator. Elizabeth couldn't even form words as Sam pulled out a carton of eggs, Swiss cheese, butter, and a loaf of wheat bread.

He whistled as he set about making his breakfast, clearly in no rush to go anywhere.

"You're revolting, Sam," Elizabeth said.

He whipped around, eggs in hand. "What did I do now, Wakefield? I bought this stuff— these are my groceries. I'm not pilfering Neil's food again."

"I'm not talking about your *breakfast*, Sam." She couldn't believe him. "You just totally used that girl, then blew her off, and now you're stuffing your face like you did nothing wrong."

"Can I eat breakfast in peace, please?" he asked, grabbing a bowl and cracking the eggs into it.

"You didn't even have the decency to drive the girl home. '*Take this bus, then transfer, then walk five miles, and you'll be right there!'* You're disgusting."

Sam beat the eggs. "Look, you told me not to lecture you on your love life, so lay off mine, okay?"

"You're not having a love life. You're having a *sex* life."

"So?" Sam asked as he poured the eggs into a skillet. "What's wrong with that?"

She glared at him. "What's wrong is that you acted like you were crazy about her last night. Then you got what you wanted, which, by the way, I had the misfortune of overhearing this morning, and then you totally blew her off—and none too gently."

He moved to the toaster and dropped four slices of bread in the slots. "*Whatever,* Elizabeth. Aren't you always telling me to mind my own business? Why don't you mind yours?"

Because it's guys like you who give good *guys a bad name,* Elizabeth wanted to scream at him. *It's guys like you who make girls nervous about trusting their hearts and their bodies to the good ones. Good ones like Finn. How could any girl feel ready to make love for the first time when she sees how jerks like you can be?*

She sighed and dropped her spoon into her cup. "I guess it's her own fault, maybe," Elizabeth said. "If she couldn't see through your phony baloney, it's her fault for believing what she wants. You, really nice? You, buying a CD because a song reminded you of her? The only remotely Sam-Burgess-like thing you did last night was to get her name wrong. So either you put on one hell of an act for those 'amazing thirteen days' or she's just really stupid."

"She's definitely not stupid," Sam said. "I think she's really cool, actually. I'm just not into getting involved with her. I've been wanting to get her into bed since the first time I saw her."

You're a pig, she thought, seething. "So why not just be honest? Why pretend you're practically in love with her?"

"Elizabeth," Sam said, sliding his omelet from the pan onto a plate. "If I'd told her I just wanted to have sex with her and not get into some relationship, do you think she'd sleep with me? No way. Girls like that don't have one-night stands. So a guy's gotta put on a little show. It's not like I'm the only one who does it. All guys do."

Not all *guys,* she corrected mentally. "So that makes it okay?" she asked, staring into her yogurt cup.

He plucked his toast next to the eggs, then grabbed the butter and a fork and sat down across from her. "It's a little too early in the morning for me to defend myself. Can I eat, please?"

"Stuff your face for all I care. Just tell me one

thing. What are you going to do when you see her in class next week? Just act like last night and this morning never happened? Barely speak to her?"

"Of course I'll speak to her," Sam told her, chewing his toast. The smell of freshly brewed coffee suddenly overtook the kitchen, and Sam shot up to pour himself a mug. "I told you, I do like her—a lot, actually. But I was and will still be more interested in sleeping with her than having a relationship. I'll just explain as nicely as I can that I realized I wasn't ready to get serious."

Elizabeth got up to pour herself a cup of coffee too. Sam dribbled milk into her mug, then his, then put the carton back into the refrigerator. "She won't think that's a little convenient?" Elizabeth asked. "That you just happened to realize that *after* you had sex with her."

They sat back down, and Sam dumped a pile of sugar into his mug. "Elizabeth, I know this isn't going to sound very nice, but that's not my problem."

"I guess not," she snapped.

"Look, Liz, it's not like she was a virgin or anything. If she were, I probably wouldn't have gone within two feet of her. Even *I'm* not that much of a dog."

Virginity was a subject that Elizabeth *did* not want to get into with Sam. He already knew too much about her own personal life.

She slid off the stool and dropped her cup in

the sink. "Well, I have a class to get to. Thanks for the vile conversation, Sam. It's been a pleasure. Next time you bring a girl here, believe me, I'll find some way to warn her about you before she gets anywhere near your bedroom."

"You can try, Wakefield, but that's what's so wonderful about girls. They only believe what they want. And if a girl really likes a guy, she'll believe whatever he says."

Elizabeth rolled her eyes. "So after all is said and done, knowing you used that girl, knowing you'll have to deal with the hassles when you see her next week, are you really going to tell me it's worth going to all the trouble in the first place just to have sex? It sounds like a lot of work."

He glanced up at her. "You know what, Elizabeth? It *wasn't* worth it. She was pretty inexperienced. So, yeah, it was a lot of work for something that wasn't even great."

Elizabeth marched to the door and shook her head. "I hope you choke on your toast."

"Oh my God!" Val stared wide-eyed at Chloe as she recounted her experience in the cafeteria. "I can't believe you did it, Chloe, I really can't. So what happened after the kiss?"

Chloe had tried to brush it off as no big deal. But with Val sitting on the bed across from her, leaning forward in rapt attention, it wasn't easy to play down the experience. Besides, Chloe always did like to inject a little drama into the stories she told.

"Oh, his girlfriend totally had her claws out. I mean, the hair on her back was literally standing on end. *Meeerowwwwrrrr!*" Chloe bared her teeth and for a split second pantomimed a catfight. "She grabbed my hair and then hurled me backward into Johanna and Lindsay. It was *so great!*"

Truth be told, Chloe was profoundly relieved to be in the safety of her dorm room, telling her story in the past tense to her best friend.

"So what did *they* do? Johanna and Lindsay, I mean. Did they step in and explain or anything?" Val wondered aloud.

"Are you kidding?" Chloe smirked. "They practically pushed me back into the cage to get mauled. If I were a lion tamer, I'd be toast right now. Johanna and Lindsay were laughing hysterically the whole time."

Val's face softened into a look of genuine concern. "Oh, Chloe, you must have been totally humiliated."

Chloe was about to break down and admit the true emotions she had been feeling. But she caught herself just in time. There was no way she was going to risk giving credence to Val's doubts about becoming a Theta. Val needed Chloe by her side too much.

"*Humiliated*? No way! It was the biggest thrill of my life! You should have seen the girlfriend's face, not to mention Mike Simmons. I mean, truthfully, I think he was kind of into the kiss."

Val tilted her head in mild disbelief. "Into it? Are you sure?"

Chloe pretended to take offense at her friend's skepticism. "Yeah. Seriously, look at me, Val. I'm a future Theta, and I'm totally hot." Chloe was only half joking since she had to admit that the experience—once it was over—had given a much needed boost to her confidence. She had kissed Mike Simmons, after all. That was the bright side.

Val giggled enthusiastically. Chloe couldn't help thinking her confidence, however fake, was contagious. She was about to pour it on even thicker, but their conversation was interrupted as the door flew open. In rushed Moira Pierce, Chloe's incredibly horrible roommate. And she was crying hysterically.

A look of concern returned to Val's face as she practically leaped from Moira's bed to give her space. Chloe wasn't so free and easy with her sympathy. Especially since Moira and her friends had always gone out of their way to make Chloe feel like dirt. "What's the matter, Moira?" she asked, sounding more irritated than compassionate.

"I just got totally humiliated in the library," Moira shrieked. "Oh my God, it was so awful!"

Val moved closer to Moira and put a gentle hand on her shoulder. "What happened, Moira? Are you all right?"

"I don't know," Moira sobbed. "I think so. I just feel like such an idiot right now."

"I'm sure you'll feel better if you talk about it," Val offered in a soft voice. "Chloe had a pretty bad experience with the Thetas too. If you guys can compare stories, maybe neither one of you will feel so bad."

Moira looked up at Chloe as if she'd just noticed Chloe was in the room. Immediately the girl's face hardened and her catlike green eyes turned ice-cold. "Well, I'd expect Chloe to get humiliated. That's her MO in life."

"It wasn't *that* bad," Chloe snapped. But apparently what happened to Moira was as bad or worse. *Good,* she thought meanly. Moira deserved it. "I just had to kiss a Sigma guy in the caf."

Moira's face softened just a bit. "That's what I had to do. It was beyond humiliating. The guy was totally gross."

Chloe stopped herself from rolling her eyes as Moira launched into a pitiful tale of being camped out in the library, studying for her history exam. She was in the same study room she always went to because that's where Brett Westphal always sat. He was the one Sigma guy she'd had a crush on all semester. And there he was, sitting next to Kyle

Parks, another Sigma guy who Moira couldn't stand because he had a face full of zits and was ugly.

In walked Lindsay and Johanna. They sat next to Moira and pulled the same whispering routine they did on Chloe in the cafeteria. Of course they ordered her to kiss Kyle—the guy she didn't like—right in front of Brett.

"So did you do it?" Val asked.

"What choice did I have?" Moira sobbed. "Of course I did. Only then they told me it wasn't good enough. 'Not enough tongue,' they said."

"'Not enough tongue'?" Chloe could barely keep herself from bursting into laughter.

"So then what happened?" Val urged Moira to finish the story.

"So then I had to kiss Brett too, as if I wasn't already humiliated enough."

Val was beginning to look downright angry. "Oh, please. Moira, tell me you didn't. . . ."

"I had to. There was nothing else I could do," Moira continued between sobs. "If I'd refused, then I'd never be a Theta."

"So what happened?" Chloe tried to sound concerned, but the question came out anxious and impatient.

"Well, before I could even kiss him, he . . . Brett . . ." Moira paused to take a breath. "He jumped out of his seat and yelled, 'Get away from me! Just get away!' And by that time everyone in the entire library was out of their seats and just staring at me like I was a loser. Me. Moira Pierce!"

Val tried to comfort Moira, telling her how sorry she was that Moira had to go through such an ordeal. Val looked at Chloe, gesturing toward Moira, whose face was still hot with tears. "You see what I mean, Chloe? All this pledge stuff is totally stupid, not to mention hurtful and demeaning to everyone involved. You know, I hate to keep saying this, but it's true. Sororities are supposed to be about support and sisterhood, not humiliation."

Once again Chloe felt like she was losing Val. In these situations she always found it best to agree with her friend. With the appropriate spin, of course.

"You're absolutely right, Val," Chloe answered emphatically. "And I'm sure it will be about that—once we're all sisters. But like I said before, pledge week is all about breaking down barriers. So that when we finally reach the end of it, we *will* be like sisters. And we *will* be there to support each other. Besides, what's a little bit of humiliation in the grand scheme of things? I mean, whatever doesn't kill you makes you stronger, right?"

Val nodded reluctantly.

"And look at the bright side," Chloe added cheerily. "We've already come this far, and in just a few more days we'll all be full-fledged Thetas."

"Yeah," Val answered without conviction, "right."

Chloe looked over at Moira, still blubbering on the edge of her bed. No matter what happened this week, she'd never feel like a sister to Moira Pierce. She thought back on all the times Moira and her snotty friends had made *her* cry. *If you ask me, Moira deserves a lot of humiliation,* Chloe thought.

The phone rang, and Chloe answered it.

"Chloe?" came the voice on the other end.

"Yes."

"This is Johanna. I want you and Val to report to Theta house immediately. There are two sisters here who require hour-long massages. And make it quick. You know how we hate to wait."

Chapter
Eight

Todd sat attentively on a bar stool in Frankie's. It was afternoon, before the place got busy, and right before Todd's early shift. Cathy, the blond bartender, leaned across the bar from the other side in a tight white T-shirt and faded Levi's. Between them lay an application for Orange County College.

For a split second Todd wondered if he should be the one applying to OCC. Without a doubt the girls he met from there were always cooler than the ones he encountered at SVU. And of course tuition was about ten times cheaper at OCC too. So as long as he was going to be in school only part-time, he'd have to consider it. But since his parents had already paid for a full load at SVU, he figured the least he could do was finish the two courses that remained on his schedule.

Of course, the application wasn't for him. It was for Cathy. Todd was just helping her fill it out.

"So, it's really called an AA degree?" Todd asked with a grin. "That's so funny—a bartender going for an AA."

"It's not that kind of AA, silly." Cathy picked up the application and swatted Todd across the top of his head. "It stands for associate-in-arts degree, and it's so I can become a paralegal. Now, are you going to help me fill this out or just sit there and make fun of me all night?"

"Well, I thought I'd make fun of you for a few more minutes, and then I'll help you," Todd answered slyly.

"Ha ha, very funny." Cathy set down the application again and started filling out the personal information at the top.

"I thought you wanted my help," Todd offered.

"I do, but I think I can handle this part myself." Cathy put a checkmark in the box labeled Nonmatriculated.

"Nonmatriculated. That means part-time, right?" Todd asked.

"That's right, genius," Cathy teased. "I wanted to go full-time, but I just can't afford it right now."

"Really? But I thought you lived with your parents," Todd blurted out, regretting the words as soon as they came out of his mouth.

Cathy looked at him crossly. "I live with my mom, Todd. I haven't seen my dad for about fifteen years."

"Oh, I'm sorry. I didn't mean—"

Cathy cut Todd off without acknowledging his lame attempt at an apology. "My mom had to support me pretty much by herself from the time I was ten years old, and now she just lost her job. So not only do I have to cover the rent all by myself now, but I'll also have to pay my own tuition . . . *if* I get in."

"Oh, man, that totally sucks," Todd offered sympathetically. He now felt like a complete idiot. But then he remembered Sam and thought he might be able to redeem himself. "Oh, hey. I just thought of something. I know this guy who's going to OCC right now. Maybe he could give you some advice or something. . . . Not like you need it. I mean, I'm sure you'll get in, no problem. But I was just thinking, he's having a party at his house this Saturday. So maybe I could take you over there and you could talk to him."

Cathy no longer looked cross. She was fuming.

"Are you kidding?" she demanded. "Like I have time for parties! I have to work a double shift on Saturday because I need the money so bad. And you're talking about parties?"

Todd wished he could somehow crawl beneath

his bar stool and disappear. He certainly felt small enough to fit under there. He must have looked it too. Because Cathy's face softened, and she gently touched his arm.

"Oh, I'm sorry for snapping, Todd. It's just that I've been so stressed out lately. And working so much. I think it's all really starting to get to me."

"I'm the one who should apologize," Todd countered sheepishly. "I feel like such a jerk. What was I thinking?"

Cathy gave his arm a light squeeze. "Oh, no, honey. You're not a jerk. I know you were just trying to be helpful. And you are. It's just that . . . I don't know. . . . You just seem so lucky, like you don't have to worry about anything. You have two parents who love you and support you. Everything has been so difficult for me lately. And I look at you, and you're just, like, blessed."

Yeah, right, Todd thought. *Just wait till my parents find out I've turned part-time.* He could feel a cloud of gloom settling over his face.

"Ah, look at you. I'm sorry." Cathy brushed a wisp of hair away from Todd's eyes. "Now I've upset *you.*"

"Don't worry about it," Todd answered with a shrug. "I'm all right. It's just that sometimes I wonder what I'm supposed to be doing with my life."

"Don't worry about that," Cathy reassured

him. "Everything is going to fall into place for you—I know it is. I mean, everyone at Frankie's thinks you're great, you know. You're smart; you're funny. You're obviously a hard worker. And you're just a totally cool guy, especially for an SVUer."

Somehow Cathy's closing words were the greatest compliment of all for Todd. A smile returned to his face as he thought about how great things were for him at Frankie's. Not only was he appreciated for who he was—everyone made such a big deal over him—but he was also making good money. His *own* money.

Nina sat with Elizabeth in the sterile waiting room of the SVU health center. Elizabeth was so nervous, Nina almost felt like she should be holding her friend's hand as a show of support. Who would have ever thought it? Nina wondered. Elizabeth Wakefield meeting with a doctor to discuss birth control.

Nina had always suspected that Elizabeth would wait for her wedding night. That is, if there was a single man out there who was willing to wait for a wedding. But beyond the surprisingly sudden interest in sex, Nina figured that inquiring about birth control before the first time was classic Elizabeth. Explore every angle, all the potential consequences, before doing anything.

That was why Nina had been so shocked that it hadn't been Elizabeth's idea to head to the health center. Elizabeth had called her this morning in some sort of panic about the subject of sex and guys, and it had taken a half hour of conversation for Nina to realize that Elizabeth was actually contemplating sleeping with her new boyfriend, Finn, a guy Nina hadn't met yet.

So when Nina had asked her what birth control she planned to use if she *did* decide to sleep with him, Nina had been stunned to learn that Elizabeth hadn't even thought about it. Nina herself had made the appointment for Elizabeth the second they'd hung up, then she'd called Elizabeth back and told her to meet her there.

The walls of the waiting room were covered with posters addressing the concerns of the day. AIDS, STDs, unwanted pregnancy, alcoholism, depression, drugs, date rape.

"I never realized how many of society's problems are related to sex," Elizabeth said, looking at the posters. "Except for drugs and alcohol, I guess."

"But drugs and alcohol are often what lead to sex in the first place," Nina pointed out.

Elizabeth stared down at the floor. Nina knew this must be a scary experience for her friend. It was one thing to start thinking about having sex for the first time. It was quite another to realize there were a lot of important things to think about and consider before making love.

"So, Nina, speaking of sex and drugs, don't you think it's about time you told me about this new rock-and-roll boyfriend of yours? From what you told me over the phone this morning, he sounds amazing."

Nina laughed. She'd been dying to talk about Xavier, but she didn't want to hog the conversation just in case Elizabeth wanted to talk about Finn. "I think 'boyfriend' may be too strong a term to use just yet," Nina began. She could feel herself starting to gush as she thought of the sexy singer. "But we did have a pretty steamy evening at Starlights on Monday night."

"I'm listening." Elizabeth's eagerness told Nina that she desperately needed something to take her mind off the business at hand. Her friend had been wringing her hands ever since they'd met outside the health center.

Now that Xavier had popped into her life, Nina was thinking that maybe it was time for her to consider birth control too. "Xavier. Wow. I don't know where to begin." Nina could feel herself beaming at the mere thought of him. "So, did I tell you how amazing his band is?"

"Um, yeah, I think so," Elizabeth answered. "But I'm not completely sure if it's sunk in yet."

"Well, they're totally great. I mean, they're all

really talented. And their songs are so good. And Xavier, he can really sing. And not just his singing, but the words are fantastic. He's so smart and clever and sensitive. And sexy. Did I tell you how sexy he is? My goodness."

Nina didn't wait for an answer from Elizabeth. Now that she was rolling down Xavier lane, she couldn't stop herself. "And the way he moves to the music. It's like he's in a trance or something. And then it was like he put *me* in a trance. I swear I could not take my eyes off him. Yet I was still totally connected to the music. And that's what he told me after the show, that he could tell I could really feel their music. That I understood what they were doing. And when he looked at me. Up onstage. Me in the audience. It was like we connected, you know what I mean?"

Elizabeth nodded. She seemed content to listen. Which was fine with Nina because she felt like she could talk about Xavier and Wired all afternoon.

"Yeah, it was like we made this psychic connection. I know that sounds totally corny, but it's true. I mean, he even said it after the show. And when he first looked at me in the audience, I thought I was imagining it. I thought that with all the lights shining in his face and with all the people in the crowd, he couldn't possibly see me. But he did. He told me. After the show he told me he was waiting for me. To meet me. To talk to me."

"So what did you talk about?" Elizabeth asked, probably wanting to get beyond Nina's talk of mystical vibes and psychic connections.

"Oh, everything," Nina responded, with no signs of slowing down. "His family, his childhood. Did I tell you his dad is a research scientist? He's actually working on a cure for cancer, if you can believe it. And Xavier is just so interesting. So not what you'd suspect from a guy who sings in a band like that. Not what you'd expect from any guy, really. I mean, he doesn't even have a TV."

"What?" Elizabeth's eyes widened. "No TV? What does he do all day? Read books?"

"I guess so." Nina spoke wistfully. "He reads, he writes, he draws. He must spend a lot of time on his music. I just can't believe I met him. Me, Nina Harper, total nerd, hanging out and partying with a hot guy in a hot band. Backstage at Starlights on a Monday night. Instead of studying for my calculus exam. It's crazy!"

"Wow, Nina, I'm so happy for you. It's almost like you're a whole new person." Elizabeth stopped herself. "Don't get me wrong. I don't mean that in a bad way. I mean, of course you're the same incredible Nina. It's not like you've changed that much. It's just so great to see you having so much fun. And you deserve it, Nina. You really do."

Nina smiled thoughtfully, still thinking of her and Xavier on the couch. Talking, kissing. "Yeah, I guess I do deserve it, huh?"

"Totally," Elizabeth answered with certainty. "So, when are you going to see him again?"

For the first time that afternoon a sense of doubt intruded on Nina's fairy-tale merry-go-round. "Well, I gave him my number, but he hasn't called me yet."

"Really?" Elizabeth sounded shocked but tried to compensate with a lame joke. "Maybe he doesn't have a phone either."

Nina admitted to herself that she was concerned over the lack of a phone call. But she was still willing to give Xavier the benefit of the doubt. "I'm sure he's just really busy. You know, with rehearsals and promoting the band and everything. Anyway, I know I'll see him Saturday when Wired plays Starlights again. And maybe I'll even bring him to the party at your house after."

Elizabeth gave Nina a huge smile, a welcome signal that her nervousness over the birth-control issue might be easing up. "You should definitely bring him to the party. He sounds so amazing, I can't wait to meet him!"

"He is completely amazing, Liz. I mean, listen to me. Even though Xavier and I have only been together once, I feel like I could go on and on and on about him. But now I want to hear about *your* new man. Finn, the sexy med student."

"What haven't I told you already?" Now it was Elizabeth's turn to gush. "Sexy, obviously. Med student, check."

"Meaning, future doctor," Nina pointed out rhetorically.

"Precisely." Elizabeth's voice wavered again. Nina was sure it was the mention of *doctor,* another reminder of exactly where they were and why. But the bubbles returned to her tone as she went on about Finn. "And not just a future doctor, but did you know that his true love is painting?"

"Ooh, an artiste." Nina smiled in acknowledgment of their shared interest in the arts.

"And of course I told you what a fantastic cook he is," Elizabeth continued, as if going down a list of prerequisites for the perfect husband. "And not only that, but he knows how to dine out too."

"Meaning?" Nina didn't quite follow.

"Meaning, he just seems to know exactly what to do in every situation. Like at dinner he was so comfortable and confident with the waiter. Ordering the perfect wine, getting a selection of appetizers so we could taste a bit of everything. And just the way he carries himself. He's so . . . I don't know, mature."

"And smart too," Nina added. "Is he, like, a total brainiac?"

"Well, of course he's smart. I mean, I don't think they accept stupid people into med school," Elizabeth answered. "But it's not like he flaunts his intelligence at all. And the same goes for everything about him. His family is obviously wealthy, he's been to the best schools, and he's completely cultured."

Elizabeth sighed, a dreamy expression on her face. "But unless any of that happened to come up in conversation or a specific situation," she continued, "you wouldn't necessarily know it. Of course you could guess it from the way he carries himself. But he's just not one to brag about things. He's just really . . . easy. It's just so easy to be with him. I always feel safe, and I always feel comfortable. And even though he's this amazing person, he never makes me feel inadequate for just being me."

Nina stopped her. "Listen, Elizabeth, there is absolutely no way that you should ever feel inadequate for being yourself. This guy sounds great; don't get me wrong. But you're quite a catch yourself, you know."

Elizabeth reached out and touched Nina's arm. "Thanks, Nina. I know. It's just that . . . well, Finn is just so wonderful. Sometimes I wonder if I even deserve him."

"Of course you do, Liz. You deserve the best of everything. You really do. And I must admit, it does sound like Finn is exactly that."

"He is, but . . ." Elizabeth appeared distracted again as her sentence trailed off into the air.

"But what?" Nina pressed.

Elizabeth hesitated. "But, well . . . I don't know. Finn is incredible. And who knows if I'll ever meet another guy like him, but I still just don't think I'm ready."

"Ready to commit? Ready for a relationship? Ready for what?" Nina was perplexed.

"Ready for sex," Elizabeth answered bluntly. "I know I'm being hopelessly old-fashioned. And probably a total idiot. But I'm just not sure I want to give up my virginity yet. And then there's Sam . . ."

Now Nina was completely perplexed. "Sam?" she asked sharply. "What *about* Sam?"

"Oh, no, no, no." Elizabeth rushed her response. "It's just that, well, I told you that whole story about him and that girl Anna this morning, right? Just the way he so casually slept with her. Like it was nothing. Like it was just another thing to do. Another babe to bag. And she's probably at home, daydreaming about Sam right now. Thinking he was probably just tired this morning, that he'll definitely call. I mean, what if Finn is really just like Sam and I'm just another one of his conquests?"

"Don't be ridiculous, Liz," Nina chastised her friend. "First of all, Finn is about ten times more mature than that jerk Sam. And most guys don't play the kind of childish games your slacker house-mate does. Besides, you're in love with Finn, aren't you? You told me that the two of you are exclusive now, right?"

"Yes . . . ," Elizabeth answered reluctantly. Her face was flushed, and a look of confusion overtook her eyes. "I mean, I don't know. I think I'm in love, but . . . everything is just so much. Maybe I'm not ready for birth control after all. I certainly don't feel ready for sex."

Suddenly the nurse appeared from behind the counter. "Miss Wakefield, the doctor will see you now."

"Hey, Todd, feel like helping me out with the books again? I'm stuck on something."

Todd quickly stood up from stocking the mixers shelf below the bar and spun around to see his manager, Rita, standing behind him. Her long, red, curly hair was pinned up, and she was wearing her glasses. He could tell she'd been poring over the ledger—she had that frustrated expression that told him she was exasperated.

"Sure!" he told her. He had just finished stocking the entire bar. All the bottled beer was on ice, the liquor shelf was replenished and thoroughly dusted, and all the mixers were in order. Sweat glistened above his brow and was beginning to show through his baggy gray T-shirt. Sitting down in the back room and doing paperwork would be a break.

"Tell you the truth," Rita said, "I'm glad you're taking on extra shifts—you've become pretty indispensable here. If I'd known I'd be getting a ledger whiz in addition to a hardworking back-bar guy, I would have breathed a lot easier."

"Wow, thanks." Todd modestly shoved his hands into the front pockets of his new jeans. "I really like helping out. Just let me wash my hands, and I'll be right there."

Todd washed his hands and went to the back office, where Rita kept the books. He sat down with her behind the big, cluttered desk and immediately figured out the crucial error that had been made. After that it took only about ten minutes for him to fix the problem.

Before he made it out the door, Rita stopped him. "Wait a second."

Todd turned around in the doorway. "Yeah, what is it?"

Rita shut the large accounting book and looked Todd in the eyes. "Since you did such a great job with the books tonight, I was wondering if you could maybe come by on Monday afternoon—before your shift—and I can train you on the books so you can take care of it when I'm not around. It should only take a couple of hours."

"Yeah, sure!" Todd answered excitedly. "No problem."

Cool! he thought. Whenever Rita asked Todd to do something for her, she always made it seem like he was the only person who could do the job. Once again he was feeling wanted and needed at Frankie's. And it was satisfying in a way that his experience at SVU never was.

He froze for a second. SVU. If he came in early on Monday, he'd have to miss the two classes he was still taking. . . .

"Todd?" she asked, peering at him. "Problem with Monday?"

He looked at her, at the approving look in her eyes. Rita and everyone at Frankie's made him feel like he was so intelligent, so capable. They never treated him like he was just some college kid who didn't know anything about the real world.

So what if I miss those classes? he thought. *I'm coming in early to work my brains on the books. That's school in itself.*

"I'll be here," he told Rita. "You can count on me!"

Chapter Nine

Chloe and Val sat with Moira and Stacey Bremerton, another pledge, along one side of a big table in the student-center cafeteria. On the opposite side sat four Theta sisters: Lindsay, Johanna, Deirdre, and Hillary.

Chloe tried not to look too anxious as she glanced at the girls on either side of her and then across the table at her tormentors. She braced herself for another round of public humiliation. Luckily she didn't see any Sigma guys around. But there were plenty of other random people in the cafeteria. And a lot of them looked eager to witness the latest Theta hazing ritual. It was almost like that was the only reason they were there. Like rubberneckers gathered at a highway accident.

Chloe was definitely nervous. But she took solace in the reality that she wasn't half as freaked as

Val. Val's hands were visibly trembling, and she kept repeating a mantra of fear—under her breath, but just loud enough for Chloe to hear.

"I don't know about this. It just doesn't feel right."

"Shhh," Chloe whispered sharply to her friend. "Don't worry, Val. It's not as bad as it seems. All you'll have to do is one outrageous thing, and then it will all be over." For the time being anyway.

Somehow her words didn't seem to be sinking in. The trembling didn't stop. And neither did the mantra of fear. Chloe hoped that Val would be picked first just so she could get it over with. And stop acting like such a wreck.

But such was not the case.

"Moira Pierce," Lindsay announced in an icy tone. "Please stand up."

Moira stood up stiffly and pushed back her chair. Chloe detected a slight tremble in her usually controlled roommate as well.

"Okay, Moira," Lindsay continued. "Since you had such a hard time kissing a Sigma guy on the lips in the library the other day, we're going to try something a little bit different today."

Moira nodded. Chloe could already see her face filling with crimson.

Lindsay pointed across the room to a table populated by slacker and hipster guys. Most of

116

them were done eating and just hanging out, joking among themselves and waiting to see what would happen at the Theta table. "Those are the 'men' of Delta Phi. Otherwise known as the freak fraternity. Now, since there is no one here today representing the prestigious Sigma fraternity, you're going to have to settle for those losers. And since I wouldn't even force a pitiful pledge to kiss a Delta Phi guy on the lips, you're going to have to kiss them somewhere else."

Lindsay paused dramatically in her condescending address before concluding with, "You will kiss each and every one of them on the feet."

Moira made a face like she had just swallowed a gulp of sour milk.

"Do not disrespect your elders with such impudent facial expressions," Lindsay snapped. "Or you will not have the privilege of kissing the feet of Delta Phi. For your pledging days will be history. Is that understood?"

Moira nodded and smiled as best she could.

Lindsay turned to the Thetas on either side of her. "Now, ladies, are there any further instructions you wish to add?"

Johanna spoke up. "Yes. Now, Moira, we want you to approach each of the gentlemen at that table individually. Introduce yourself, kneel before them, and then request the honor of kissing their feet. Once you have kissed their feet—and remember, you don't have to use your tongue this time because we're feeling oh so merciful—then you shall stand again before approaching the next boy."

Moira nodded again as the red in her cheeks became more brilliant by the second. Chloe couldn't help smiling at the chance to witness Moira's complete and utter disgrace.

"Now, Moira," Johanna added. "If any boy at that table refuses your advances, you must throw yourself at his feet, wrap both arms around his ankles, and scream at the top of your lungs, 'Why? Why won't you let me kiss your feet?' Is that understood?"

Moira nodded once more and walked slowly toward the table across the room.

After kissing just three sets of feet Moira was near tears and the entire table of Delta Phi guys was in hysterics. The Theta sisters looked on approvingly. And Chloe, Val, and Stacey watched in horror. Nearly half the cafeteria was out of their seats to see what was going on.

After Moira had thoroughly shamed herself and returned to the table without a shred of dignity, Lindsay pointed at Val. "Okay, Johanna, what do we have in store for Ms. Val?"

"Hmmm." Johanna pretended to ponder. "Well, Val, since we're all so fond of you, we're going to let you off easy. No kissing for you today.

118

What we'd like for you to do is a simple public-service announcement. Now, stand up."

Val slowly stood and glanced nervously around the room.

Johanna stood as well and pointed to a table in the corner where a heavyset girl was eating by herself. Chloe noticed that they were pointing at Deena, Val's roommate. "Okay, Val, do you see the hungry hippo over there? The one scarfing down that ice cream sundae like there's no tomorrow?"

Val obviously recognized her roommate and was now fuming. Her cheeks were beet red, and a sour frown was plastered to her face. She shook her head slowly, unable to respond with words.

"Do you see her or don't you?" Johanna demanded.

"Yes," Val responded with pursed lips. "Yes, I see her."

"Good," Johanna answered smugly. "Now, from where you are standing, I want you to tell that big, happy girl, in a voice loud enough for her and everyone else in this room to hear, that she should be ashamed of herself for eating ice cream in public when she's so fat, she can barely fit in her chair."

A look of horror consumed Val's face. She flashed a steely stare at Johanna and the other

Thetas and continued shaking her head. Slowly. Back and forth.

It was obvious to Chloe that Val wasn't going to go through with it. *Come on, Val,* Chloe urged her silently. *Just do it. So what if she's your room-mate? I mean, sure, it's a little mean. But I'm sure she'll understand when you explain everything later. You have to do this, or you'll never be a Theta. Come on, Val. Don't be stupid.*

Chloe desperately wanted her friend to perform the stunt and get into Theta alongside her. And frankly, she didn't care much for Deena in the first place. Val's roommate had always acted somehow superior to Chloe. And now, just as had happened with Moira, it was payback time. But even while Chloe urged her friend to go through with it, at least inside her own head, she wasn't going to say anything out loud. For one thing, that was up to the Theta sisters. And for another, Chloe didn't want to risk turning her one good friend against her.

Val sat down again without saying anything.

"We're waiting, Val," Johanna stated impatiently, tapping her fingers on the tabletop.

Finally Val spoke. "I'm sorry, but I'm not going to do it."

"And why is that?" demanded Johanna.

"Because that isn't just some random girl. And even if she were, I still wouldn't do it," Val answered matter-of-factly.

"Oh, yeah?" Johanna was taken aback by Val's attitude. So were the rest of the Thetas. And the pledges. "So, who is she?"

"Her name is Deena, and she happens to be my roommate. She's also my friend."

"Oh, well, well, well. Your roommate *and* your friend," Lindsay spoke up sarcastically. "I guess this is the time for you to choose, Val. Between your so-called roommate and friend and the brightest future at SVU you could ever imagine. Now, would you like to soar with the sisterhood or wallow with the pigs?"

Chloe looked hopefully at Val, wishing she could finally let go of dowdy Deena and stick with her. Her and the coolest sorority on campus. But Chloe knew that Val had already chosen. So she merely hoped that they could still be friends, if not sisters.

Tears welled in Val's eyes as she stood up from the table one final time. "You know, I'm actually glad I got to experience this disgusting little display of sisterhood," Val announced, directing her venom at Lindsay and Johanna and the other Thetas. "Because now I know what Theta is really all about. And I for one do not want to join a sorority that encourages such nasty, hurtful behavior, no matter how you care to justify it. I've made my choice. I'm outta here."

As Val began to walk away, all the eyes at the table turned to Chloe.

*   *   *

Elizabeth trailed her fingers around the number pad on the phone, the dial tone humming on and on in her ears. She didn't even hear it anymore until the tone broke and a horrible voice came over the wire, saying, "If you'd like to make a call, please hang up now. . . ." She hung up. She didn't want to make a call. She just wanted to talk to her boyfriend. Nothing major, just to know what's up, how his test went, *are you still so sweet?* She smoothed her bedspread with her hands. Nothing major.

The little bag she had bought at the pharmacy lay empty and flattened before her on the bed. One small box of latex condoms, unopened; one small, white, square receipt; one large bottle of nail-polish remover, unopened; one pink copy of a physician's prescription; one medium-sized square cardboard box containing one month's supply of birth-control pills. Unopened.

Elizabeth traced lines on her bedspread between her purchases. She stared at them like she was studying for a test. Suddenly she felt tired. She looked at herself in the mirror above her dresser. Why was she just sitting here? She picked up the bottle of nail-polish remover and went into the bathroom.

It would be so much easier if Finn would call *her*. Then she could be happy to hear from him, and she wouldn't sound clingy or whiny. And then she could tell him what the doctor had said because he would ask her what's new. And then she could tell him that the pills wouldn't be effective for another month, and he would understand that, and she could joke about biochemistry.

Which would all be easier than trying to find a place for a large bottle of nail-polish remover on her small bathroom shelves, already packed with beauty products. She opened the nearly empty bottle and poured some in from the new one, and then she put the nearly full bottle under the sink. Her hands were shaking.

She thought about the contraceptive-effectivity rates of condoms and the pill versus condoms alone. Finn would appreciate the numerical precision. Maybe he would suggest that they wait until the pill became effective. Right. No way. He would have ten answers for that.

They needed to talk, that was for sure. But Elizabeth also just needed to hear his voice. There was something so reassuring about the way her name sounded from him. But then, they also needed to discuss their options.

Had Finn been tested for HIV? The doctor at the clinic warned her that some guys were very reluctant to use a condom sometimes and that she had to insist. But she and Finn were exclusive. No, she was the only virgin in the relationship, so they were supposed to talk about his sexual history. Right. *That* sounded fun.

Maybe she shouldn't go on the pill, so that they would have to use condoms. That would be easier. Or she could tell Finn that she wasn't on the pill, so that he would have to use condoms. But what was she thinking about? That was lying! They were going to use condoms at least until Finn had a test for HIV, and at least for the first month, and then . . . and then . . . Elizabeth didn't know. She didn't know what she was doing. Suddenly she was scared again.

Elizabeth walked back into her bedroom and put the condoms and the pills in her purse. *Might as well have everything ready,* she thought. She knew that she and Finn had plans to go to his place after the party the next night. She didn't know what was going to happen. But there was no way that she was going to stay home with him, so there was no point in leaving the condoms here. And as for the pill, well, she just wanted to hang on to those a little while longer. *Just a little more time,* she thought. *A little while longer.*

She was afraid to go on the pill. The doctor had explained that the hormones in the pill would simulate her body being pregnant, which basically meant that her body wouldn't let her get pregnant "again." But it had no effect in preventing sexually transmitted diseases. That was where the condoms came in. But if they had to use condoms anyway, then why did she have to go on the pill too?

Because condoms don't always work to prevent pregnancy, she thought. *But if the condom doesn't keep the sperm out of me, how can it work well enough to protect me from getting a disease?*

Elizabeth's stomach was turning upside down and back, over and over, like a little gymnast inside her. She felt like she was going to cry.

Sitting back down on the bed, she composed herself. *It's not that big a deal,* she told herself. *People make these decisions all the time. I can too.* But the idea of another person in the same situation, even if it was her identical twin sister, meant nothing to her. This was too personal, too individual, for anybody else's experience to matter.

"This is ridiculous," she said to herself, and she picked up the telephone and dialed Finn's number. "We need to talk," she murmured to herself coolly, smoothing out her bedspread. "And not at the party, but now."

Finn's voice filled her with a feeling of safety. "Hello?"

"Hi, there," Elizabeth said. "It's me."

"Hi, 'me,'" Finn said. "How's it going?"

"Fine," she said, and was quiet. *So much for talking about it,* she thought. She couldn't say a word.

"Well," Finn said, "that's great. Hey, Liz, can

125

we talk later? I have a study group over, and we've got to get back to physiology."

Elizabeth groaned inwardly. No! "Um, Finn? I went to the doctor recently."

"What's wrong?" Finn sounded concerned.

"Nothing!" Elizabeth tried to sound extra sunny. "Nothing's wrong. Nothing! I'm fine!"

"Well, that's great. Say, like I said, I really have to get back to the books now. . . ." Elizabeth heard a rumbling sound and then a thump; Finn's voice trailed away, as if he had dropped the phone.

Elizabeth cupped the phone closer to her ear. "Finn?" she called. He didn't say anything. There was a loud rustling from his end of the phone and the sound of another person's voice, obviously female. What was she saying? Was that laughter?

Finn's voice came back on the line. "Sorry, Liz, I dropped the phone. Uh, listen, I really can't keep my classmates waiting. Was there anything else?"

"Oh, Finn, can't we just talk a little while longer?" Elizabeth pleaded.

"How's everything set for tomorrow?" he asked.

"Fine," she said. She didn't know what to say. She didn't want to talk about the party! She didn't want to talk about condoms either. She didn't want to talk about sex at all. She didn't even want to talk. She wanted Finn to talk to her.

"All right!" he said heartily. "So we're on, right?"

"Right," she said.

"So, uh, good, we're set for tomorrow, and I can't wait to see you!"

There was a little ruckus in the background. She heard the female voice again, this time giggling. "Finn," she asked. "Who's that?"

"I told you—a study group from physiology. Big test coming up!"

"It doesn't sound like they're studying to me," Elizabeth said.

"That's because they're waiting for me to get back. Look, Liz, I just can't talk any longer. Everything'll be all right tomorrow, I promise. Okay?"

"Okay," Elizabeth said. She was entirely unassured. She felt like she could have been talking to anyone. Even Sam listened better. But what did she expect? She wasn't even willing to say what she needed to. She was just going to have to wait. Everything would be all right tomorrow. Finn always made her feel so safe, she would be able to discuss everything openly, intelligently. She started to feel a little better.

"Okay, then! Bye, Liz."

"Bye," she whispered.

She heard the line click. She felt like crying. "We need to talk," she repeated to nobody. She sat on her bed, the phone in her hand, smoothing the same spot on her bedspread over and over. Then the phone crackled, and a voice came on the line: "If you'd like to make a call, please hang up and dial again. If you need assistance, please hang up and dial your operator."

Elizabeth hung up the phone and buried her face in her pillow.

Chloe was on the spot. Lindsay, Johanna, Deirdre, and Hillary were all staring at her. So were Moira and Stacey, the other two pledges. Even Val was sticking around to see what Chloe would do. This was her chance. She'd have to accept whatever challenge the Thetas dished out. And she would rise to the occasion to prove that she was Theta material. Somehow she guessed what was coming next.

"Okay, Chloe," Lindsay snapped. "If your overly sensitive little friend won't do it, then I guess that leaves you. Now, stand up and tell that fat chick she ought to be ashamed of herself for eating ice cream in public."

Chloe glanced across the room at Deena, who appeared oblivious to the entire proceedings. It was true, thought Chloe, Deena should be ashamed of herself for always stuffing her face.

And how could *she* have such a superior attitude toward Chloe when she looked and acted the way she did? As if she cared nothing for how she was perceived by others. No, Chloe had never liked Deena.

And this would be the perfect opportunity to show her just how much. And if it helped her get into Theta, then that was all the better.

She had to do it. If she didn't, she'd never be a Theta. And the Thetas were her only hope of ever truly fitting in, of actually being someone, of having friends, at Sweet Valley University.

But when Chloe looked up to see Val standing near the table, waiting to see what she would do, she had another thought. In the combination of hope and dread that was written on Val's face, Chloe saw the consequences of going through with the prank. She knew that if she told off Deena, she would lose Val as a friend forever. And Val was the only friend she had at SVU.

But what was Val compared to all the friends she would have once she became a Theta? Of course she had to do it. Really, there was no other choice.

Very slowly Chloe rose from her seat. She looked across the room at Deena, who was totally lost in the bliss of hot fudge and soft vanilla ice cream. In the loudest voice she could muster, Chloe called out across the room, "Hey, Deena!"

Then she paused. Chloe first looked at Val, offering her a sheepish, sideways smile. Val shook her head once and stared at the floor in response. Then Chloe looked in the eyes of every Theta gathered around the table. She gave a smug smile to each of them, feeling suddenly powerful for facing the biggest challenge of her life. Finally she spoke.

"Hey, Deena," she repeated. "Val and I are about to go to the mall. Wanna come with us?"

Chloe didn't even glance at the Theta girls. Instead she basked in the huge smile that Deena flashed from across the room. Deena happily jumped from her seat and rushed toward Chloe, dropping her half-eaten sundae in the trash along the way.

Chloe turned to Lindsay and Johanna and the other girls. "I guess I'm outta here too," she snapped.

She turned to face Val, who was gawking at her with gaping mouth. Big smiles spread across each of their faces. The Theta sisters and pledges were goggling Chloe too. But none of them looked too pleased.

As Deena approached the table, Chloe put one arm around her shoulders and the other around Val's. The three girls walked away arm in arm, giggling all the way to the exit.

Chapter Ten

It was Saturday night at Starlights, and Nina was living it up like never before. She had gone shopping that day with Francesca and was wearing her new emerald green minidress and black, knee-high boots. The stretchy fabric clung tightly to her body, and the textured green shimmered in the pulsing lights, perfectly offsetting Nina's soft cocoa skin.

Francesca was looking as sexy as ever in a red, white, and blue Tommy Hilfiger tank top and matching navy miniskirt. Every guy in the place seemed to be staring at her. But Nina couldn't help noticing that she was getting plenty of leers and looks herself.

Wired was halfway through their first set, and Nina was psyched to be recognizing so many of their songs from Monday night. Xavier sounded great. And he was looking as hot as ever. Shirtless again, with baggy brown cords and desert boots. He moved slowly around the stage, stalking the mike stand. And when he caught it, he alternated between guttural bellows and syrupy-sweet crooning. Whatever his vocal style was at the moment, his voice and the music affected Nina the same. The heavy bass line thumped in her sternum, while Xavier's intonations pierced right through her heart.

This band is going to be so huge, thought Nina. *I can't believe I'm actually involved with the lead singer.* Someone jostling for space bumped Nina's arm, and she looked up to recognize a girl from her calculus class. Unfortunately Nina was jarred from her dance trance as her mind drifted back to the C-minus she got on that last calculus test. Bummer. But hanging out with Xavier instead of studying was way worth it, she decided. And she immediately perked up at the sight of his muscular chest on stage. Her mind drifted again, this time to more pleasant memories. Like making out backstage on Monday night.

Nina made her way to the front of the crowd and pressed up against the edge of the stage. She was anxious to reestablish that priceless eye contact with Xavier. But for some reason it wasn't working. The connection that was so clear during the last show was now as patchy as a weak signal on an AM radio. No more long stares and luscious smiles. Now the best she could get was a fleeting glance and barely an extra grin. Xavier looked like he was expending all his leftover energy looking at every other girl in the audience. Instead of at Nina.

At the end of the set Nina moved to the edge of the stage to intercept Xavier as he descended into the crowd. When he hopped down off the stage, she grabbed his arm.

"Hey, Xavier," she purred. "You guys sound absolutely amazing tonight."

"Oh, hey," he answered casually. A bit too casually for Nina's tastes. "Uh, thanks."

If there was any eye contact at all, it lasted less than a second. Xavier's dark and suddenly elusive eyes drifted out across the audience. And then, without another word, his body followed.

Nina was left wondering how this could possibly be the same person she had been with the other night—when she was so sure they had shared a deep and meaningful connection. Did he even recognize her? She couldn't take her eyes from him as he drifted through the crowd. Every pretty girl that offered a smile won his undivided attention, if only for a moment. There was such an ease to the way Xavier worked the crowd. What Nina had thought was an attentiveness reserved only for her was now being squandered on every female in sight. And she was left with nothing.

Nina watched in disbelief as Xavier made his way through the flock of girls. His sweat was literally dripping as he spread his essence through the surging room. How could he have just dissed her like that? How could he be so cold to her and so hot for everyone else in the room?

Nina stared for a minute more until she was completely overcome with anxiety. Shock quickly gave way to anger, which morphed immediately into hopeless hurt and extreme embarrassment. How could she have been so stupid to fool herself like that?

She'd thought they had something. But then all the hours they spent together on the green couch were suddenly nullified. The relationship she'd thought they established behind the stage was ground into dust on the other side of it. The public side. Nina had to get away from that spot before she broke down into tears.

Shaking and choking, she rushed toward the bathrooms at the back of the club. She forced her way through the crowd, blindly bumping anyone in her way. Their indignant stares and angry protests bounced off her as she made her way to the back. Just as she reached a clearing at the edge of the crowd, someone grabbed her from behind. Francesca.

"Nina, what's the matter?" Francesca asked with a mix of confusion and concern. "What are you running from?"

Nina's mouth could only manage one word. "Xavier."

Francesca remained calm. "Well, I hate to tell you this. But I don't think he's exactly chasing after you."

Nina composed herself enough to speak. In fragments at least. "No! I know! Didn't you see that? He barely even acknowledged me. I told him he was good. Amazing. I touched his arm. He didn't even look at me. And now he's flirting with every other girl here! I'm such an idiot. Fool. Stupid fool."

Francesca placed a firm yet comforting hand on each of Nina's shoulders, as if she had to steady her to keep her from falling. She looked her in the eyes and tried to calm her. "Nina, you've got to relax, babe. You're really overreacting here. Take it easy."

Nina stared mute, unable to speak for shame of what she had done. What she was doing. What she had thought. Everything that had been so right an hour ago was now so totally wrong. Not only had she completely fooled herself into believing her fantasy, but now she was making a scene in front of Francesca and everyone else in the club.

"Listen, Nina," Francesca continued, maintaining a hold on Nina's shoulders. "Xavier's a musician. He's in a band. They've got groupies everywhere. Just look at them. Look at all those girls vying for their attention."

"I see them, I see them." Nina moaned.

"Okay, well?" Francesca sounded less compassionate and more perturbed by the second. "They have to flirt to keep the girls into the band."

"But he could have at least acknowledged me," Nina mumbled.

"Don't worry, he will." Francesca pointed toward her own boyfriend, standing by the bar. "Look at Billy over there. See that group of girls gathered around him? He's chatting it up with all of them. I know they're cute. I know they're all into him. But I also know he's going to be coming home with me at the end of the night. So I don't even sweat it. I'm totally relaxed, and you should be too. Just don't get all possessive, Nina. Unless you prefer your old lonely lifestyle. Studying alone on a Saturday night?"

Nina was speechless. Maybe she did prefer her old lonely life. It certainly didn't include getting C's on calculus tests. Or getting blown off by a guy she had made out with for four hours straight.

In fact, Nina thought, she was perfectly happy with the way things were before. What was so bad about studying on a Saturday night anyway? She couldn't remember it ever being as unpleasant as she felt right now. Did she really like Wired's music that much? Was Starlights really as hip as everyone here thought it was? Maybe she was better off studying in the library. Wasn't that why she was going to college in the first place?

Nina forgot about Francesca for a moment and was drifting through her week's class schedule. Trying to think of the positives about school now that her party life at Starlights—and hanging out with Xavier—was over.

But all thoughts of school vanished when Nina felt the unforgettable touch of two warm, strong hands on her waist from behind. And the familiar yet undefinable scent of Xavier as his dreads brushed against her bare neck. He whispered in her ear, "Hey, beautiful, why so sad?"

Every desperate thought inside Nina's head dissolved at Xavier's touch. She effortlessly turned to face him, and he greeted her with soft, open lips. His kiss was potent but brief. Just long enough to let her know that more would follow later.

He spoke with sexy assurance. "I'll see *you* after the show. You know I can barely wait."

Nina silently answered his sultry grin with a honey-dripping smile of her own. As Xavier walked away, she watched with the same level of intensity as before. But this time it felt so much better.

Nina glanced at Francesca, who gave her a look that said, See? What did I tell you? She didn't have to say anything. Nina realized she was right. *What's my problem?* Nina asked herself. *I do have to loosen up.* She made her way back through the crowd with a new burst of energy. Relief washed over her and primed her body for a new wave of joy as Xavier took to the stage with the band.

Val and Chloe were busy unpacking their shopping bags from the Gap on Chloe's bed.

"Isn't shopping the most perfect way to get over the pain of forsaking your future?" Chloe forced a smile along with her sardonic attempt at humor.

It was true, though. Going shopping with Val and Deena did manage to take Chloe's mind off her student-center disaster. For the first time she had actually enjoyed Deena's company. Well, maybe *enjoy* was too strong a word. But at least she had found her bearable. Chloe even glimpsed a hint of what Val must see in her dowdy roommate. Deena might seem shy and quiet most of the time, but when she did speak, she was definitely outspoken. And once you got beyond her gruff, unforgiving exterior, she had a pretty great sense of humor.

So for at least a couple of hours Chloe was able to forget about removing herself from the Theta pledge class and turning her back on whatever bright future she might have had at SVU. But by the time they returned to campus, Chloe was filled with dread.

What had she done? Traded her spot in the coolest, most happening sorority on campus to spare the feelings of one girl? Choosing the friendship of Val over the entire sisterhood of Theta, including Jessica Wakefield and all her well-connected friends?

Chloe had barely spoken a word between the campus entrance and their hall in Oakley, when she said good-bye to Deena and went with Val to her room. It was still sinking in. No more pledge week. No more parties at Sigma. No more friendly hellos from Jessica and the other Theta sisters.

But now as she looked over at Val, Chloe had another thought about her decision. Maybe it was the right one after all. Being with Val had always been more fun than hanging out with any of the Theta sisters anyway. And joining Val in standing up to Lindsay and Johanna at the cafeteria had felt truly incredible. Still, Chloe couldn't ignore the sense of emptiness she felt in the pit of her stomach. No matter how glad she was to still be friends with Val, she couldn't quite manage a smile.

Val looked at Chloe expectantly. "Are you all right, Chlo?"

"I'm okay. . . ." Chloe could feel her voice cracking as she tried to stay upbeat. "I know what we did was for the best, but . . . I don't know. . . . I just think about things. . . . Like, what am I going to tell my mom? I mean, she was really counting on me becoming a Theta. You know, following in her footsteps and everything."

Val was matter-of-fact in her answer. "Just tell her what the Thetas are really like now. What they've become. I'm sure the sorority wasn't as mean-spirited and abusive when your mom was at Theta."

Chloe was reluctant to agree. "Yeah, I guess, but . . . how am I going to be friends now with Jessica and, you know, all the girls in Theta who are cool?"

Val empathized. "I know. I like a lot of the girls in Theta too. But then there are so many stuck-up, full-of-themselves, heartless, petty snobs that it's not even worth it. It's like, how do you break through to the sisters like Jessica and Denise when there are so many Lindsays and Johannas around?"

"You're right, Val." Chloe could certainly see her point. Maybe she wasn't going to cry after all. "And it did feel good to stand up to them for what was right."

"Exactly." Val punctuated Chloe's statement. "How would we have felt if we hadn't stood up for ourselves? And what if we would have joined their stupid sorority and become just like them? Torturing pledges and humiliating total strangers—how can you feel good about that?"

Val's newfound confidence was starting to rub off on Chloe. "Yeah, who needs a sorority anyway? I feel like you and I are sisters whether we're wearing matching pins or not."

Val looked at her speechlessly. She reached out and gave Chloe a big hug. "I'd take you as a sister over the Thetas any day."

Chloe and Val were still embracing when Moira sauntered in and eyed them with a look of pity and contempt. "Oh, if it isn't the self-righteous losers of SVU," she announced. "What, are you two a couple now?"

Chloe let go of Val and shot Moira a cold stare. "Excuse me?"

"Oh, nothing." Moira tried to act nonchalant. "It's just that first the two of you walk out on Theta together, and now I see you in a warm embrace. I just thought it might be some kind of social-suicide pact."

Val looked at Moira, perplexed. "Social suicide? What's that supposed to mean?"

"Oh, come on, Val. You're a smart girl—you should be able to figure it out," Moira snapped back at her. "What I mean is, your social lives are now officially over."

Chloe placed her hands on her hips and looked at Moira defiantly. "Oh, yeah? How could that be?"

Moira's voice was dripping with sarcasm. "I must have entered the wrong room. I thought you were my unfortunate roommate, Chloe Murphy. The one who just destroyed her chances of ever joining the most powerful sorority at SVU."

"Oh, so now we're doomed. Is that it?" Chloe wasn't about to admit to her roommate that she had just been thinking the exact same thing.

"I'm afraid so, my sensitive little fools." Moira heaved a sigh of disgust. "You two are such idiots. I mean, I do realize that Deena's nice and all. And she *is* Val's roommate. But *please*. Do you really think that sparing one fat girl's feelings is worth losing an entire sorority like Theta?"

Chloe was about to remind Moira of her shoe-kissing duties when they were interrupted by a sharp knock at the door. Moira yanked open the door to reveal the entire Theta government standing in the hallway: Jessica, Lila Fowler, Alexandra Rollins, and Denise Waters, the president.

Denise, as usual equipped with her pink Plexiglas clipboard, was trailing down a list of names with her pencil. "Perfect," she announced, glancing between her clipboard and the girls inside the room, "Val and Chloe are both here."

Oh, great, thought Chloe, *here comes the official you're-not-Theta-material speech.* She braced herself for being formally dismissed from the pledge class. Chloe looked toward Jessica, anxious to see how she was going to handle the situation. Would she be cold and businesslike, acting without emotion? Or would she be nasty and mean like Lindsay and Johanna? Chloe expected Jessica to be pleasant but firm. After all, they were friends, weren't they? Yet Chloe knew that as chair of pledge week, Jessica would have to enforce the rules.

But the huge smile on Jessica's face threw Chloe for a loop. As Jessica flashed her goofy grin, looking anxiously from her to Val, Chloe felt completely weirded out. *Why on earth is she so happy about kicking me out of the pledge class?* she asked herself. *I mean, I thought we were friends. The least she could do is exhibit a little regret!* Chloe huffed silently. *Maybe we're not such great friends after all.*

If Jessica was going to be so pleased about officially dropping her and Val from the Theta pledge class, Chloe wished that she could have at least done it in private. She wasn't looking forward to being further humiliated by getting dissed in front of all four Theta officers.

Now Chloe wouldn't be able to face any of them on campus either. And she wasn't exactly crazy about the idea of being terminated in front of snotty Moira. Chloe knew that from this day on, she'd never hear the end of it. In fact, she'd probably have to move to another room, if not transfer to another school altogether.

Chloe could barely take her eyes off Jessica's effervescent, smiling face, waiting for her to let loose with some sort of evil, mad-scientist laugh. But instead she just nodded toward Denise.

Denise glanced once more at her clipboard and then addressed Chloe and Val. "Girls, I am pleased to admit that pledge week is now officially over."

"Yeah," Moira said with a snort, "it's over for Chloe and Val."

"No, Moira," Jessica interjected sharply. "It's over for everyone. As of today, there will be no more Theta pledge-week activities. That is, until initiation."

"I don't understand . . . ," Chloe blurted out.

"And why are you telling this to *us*?" Val added. "Chloe and I already dropped out of the pledge class this afternoon."

Chloe shot Val a hard stare. What was she saying? Chloe hadn't dropped out. She had merely refused to participate in one of the required rituals. Sure, she had expected to be kicked out for it. But she wasn't a quitter. Chloe wanted to catch Val's eye before she said anything else to undermine her chances at salvaging her pledge nomination. But

Val was too busy looking at Jessica and Denise to notice Chloe's alarm.

Jessica responded, glancing back and forth between her and Chloe as she spoke. "I know, Val. We heard all about what happened this afternoon. And first of all, let me take this opportunity to apologize to both of you."

Huh?

Chloe was confused. Why was Jessica apologizing to them? What was happening?

Denise chimed in with her own apology and then continued where Jessica left off. "Today's incident in the student center is the main reason we've decided to put an end to pledge week," she explained. "We as Theta officers called a special meeting today, and Johanna, Lindsay, and the other sisters present at today's hazing have all been reprimanded."

"Reprimanded?" Now it was Moira's turn to act confused.

"Exactly," Jessica replied. "Theta will no longer tolerate such insensitive and demoralizing behavior among its sisters. The sorority is therefore reinstating every dismissed pledge."

Chloe's eyes lit up. "You mean we're not kicked out of the pledge class?"

"That's right, " Jessica answered with another big smile. Then her face turned serious. "But Val and Chloe, I just want to say that I hope the two of you can forgive the sisters of Theta for what's happened this week. And I hope you both still want to join us. As you can see, we need more sisters like the two of you."

Chloe could barely believe her ears. What had started out as the worst day of her life was now turning out to be the greatest. She looked over at Val, hoping to see the same relieved and joyous expression on her face. But instead Val looked even sadder than before, when they both thought they had been dropped. *What's with her?* Chloe wondered.

Chapter Eleven

If it weren't for his alarm clock, Sam probably would have slept right through the party. Sometimes it took him a while to fall asleep (especially when there was something on his mind), but once he was out, he was out cold. The only thing that could bring Sam out of a deep sleep was his trusty Sony Dream Machine. He'd had the silver, cube-shaped alarm clock as long as he could remember. And it never failed.

Sam loved naps, especially in the early evenings, right before going out. His friend Jared in Boston called them disco naps. The nap you take so you can stay out all night at the disco. Obviously a term from the seventies, Sam figured. But somehow rave nap didn't sound quite right. Sam didn't just take naps so he could party later, though. He needed them to recover from his bouts of insomnia.

Last night had been another sleepless one. Once again Sam had found himself unable to nod out. Wide awake against his will, wondering when Elizabeth would get home. And then when he heard her get home, wondering whether or not he should go out into the kitchen to talk to her. And then wondering why he didn't once she had gone off to bed. Well, he'd get to talk to her soon enough. And he'd probably get to confront the famous Finn while he was at it. From the noise outside his bedroom door, Sam could tell that the party was in full swing.

Sam flipped on the lamp and gulped down the glass of water waiting on his bedside table. He threw on some reasonably clean khakis and his favorite shirt, a black T-shirt, which smelled like Bounce. He gave himself a cursory check in the mirror and was pleased to see that his shaggy, sandy hair was perfectly disheveled. "Ladies of Sweet Valley, prepare to be dazzled," Sam said to his reflection in a tone of self-mockery that only he could fully appreciate.

Sam emerged from the familiar cocoon of his room into a brightly lit kitchen full of blabbering college kids. Every SVU peer group was represented. Frat boys and sorority girls, skaters and hip hoppers, nerds who were suddenly hip and hipsters who looked like nerds. Jocks and stoners and nondescriptoids. There was even a goth kid lurking by the back door.

Sam glanced around the room and realized that he didn't know a single person among the two dozen partyers standing in his kitchen. Noticing a smattering of beer puddles and stamped-out cigarettes on the linoleum, he ducked back in his room for a pair of shoes.

When he emerged again, Sam strode purposefully through the kitchen scene and made his way to the living room. He was certain he'd find at least one of his three housemates in there. Sure enough, across the room he spotted both Neil and Jessica, talking to a thin, good-looking guy in vintage clothes and wearing expensive glasses. Sam noticed Neil's eyes dancing about his face and watched as Jessica looked intently back and forth between Neil and his stylish friend. He was about to walk up and say hi when he caught a glimpse of the other Wakefield twin.

Elizabeth and Finn were cozy on the yellow couch, bodies tilted in a triangle, fingers interlocked, whispering sweet whatevers into each other's oh-so-attentive faces. Finn was looking so sickeningly deeply into Elizabeth's eyes that Sam was afraid he might projectile vomit all over both of them. He took a deep breath and decided to head back to the kitchen and grab a beer. Suddenly he felt like he needed one.

When Sam returned to the living room with an icy-cold one in his hand, his eyes returned to the couch where Elizabeth and Finn were sitting. Neither one of them had acknowledged him yet. And they weren't about to.

Sam watched as Finn tilted his head at Elizabeth, gesturing toward the stairs that led to the second floor—and her bedroom. Sam could see the hesitation on Elizabeth's face as she considered Finn's suggestion. She gave a coy smile and looked about the room. Before Sam could look away, Elizabeth caught his eye. Their stares locked for a fraction of a second without either of them fully registering the other.

Then, as if the sight of Sam suddenly helped to sway her, Elizabeth smiled at Finn and got up from the couch. She took his hand in hers and led him toward the stairs.

Finally Chloe was psyched. As soon as she heard the knock, she sprang from her bed and swung the door wide open. "That was fast!" she sang at the acne-challenged Domino's Pizza delivery boy standing before her, cradling a steaming cardboard box.

He certainly was a more welcome sight than the Theta squad had been an hour before. But Chloe was pleased to recall that that encounter had actually turned out all right. She and Val were back in! Hence the celebratory large pie with the works. Chloe paid the pizza boy, gave him a generous tip, and carried the warm box of cheesy goodness over to her desk.

As she opened the box, steam rose up from it and the spicy smell wafted through the room. "I hope you like sausage!" Chloe chirped as she offered up a slice to Val.

"I love just about anything on pizza!" Val tried to sound enthusiastic, but it was clearly a struggle. "Except for pineapples," she added, crinkling her nose.

Chloe noticed her friend's low mood but tried not to let it bring her down. "Ick! I know. Pineapples on pizza. That's one thing about California that I do not understand!"

Val bit hungrily into her slice, then daintily dabbed her paper napkin at the corners of her mouth. "Hey, this is pretty good."

"Only the best for new Theta sisters!" Chloe announced, raising her slice of pizza as if she were making a toast.

Val didn't respond.

Chloe opened her minifridge and pulled out two plastic bottles of diet Coke. She handed one to Val and tried again to toast their good fortune. She raised her bottle high in the air and tried to make eye contact with Val. "Here's to the new Theta era!"

Val finally looked up but only managed half a smile. She barely raised her diet Coke to take a drink.

Chloe was definitely feeling the lackluster vibe coming from her friend, but she wasn't going to give up on her plan to celebrate. "Come on, Val, don't you realize that what started out as the worst day of our lives is now the absolute greatest?"

Val just sighed.

But Chloe was undeterred. "I mean, the fact that we were reinstated is like a miracle. Not a miracle, though. It's like a sign. A sign that things are finally turning around. See, if the Theta government decides to punish the sisters who were acting so evil and then reinstates us for standing up to them, then it's got to mean that the sorority is changing for the better, right? And now that you and I are joining, Theta's going to be ten times cooler than it ever was!"

Val put down her slice of pizza and looked at Chloe reluctantly. "Chloe, I thought you already understood this. But I guess I'm going to have to come right out and say it again: I'm not joining Theta."

Chloe practically choked on her pizza at Val's confession. "What? What are you talking about, Val? Of course you're joining Theta."

Val was calm and cool in her reply. "No, Chloe, I'm not joining. I don't want to be a Theta."

"What are you talking about?" Chloe shrieked. "After everything we've been through to get where we are now? How can you just give all that up?"

"Maybe that's just it," Val answered with a sigh. "After all we've been through, I guess I realized that it's just not worth it. That joining a group that puts you through hell to get in just isn't a group I think I want to join. I don't know—maybe this whole pledge-week experience was just too much for me."

"But you wanted to be in Theta so bad," Chloe protested.

"No, Chloe, *you* wanted to be in Theta so bad. I just thought I did . . . for a while. But deep down, I think I always knew that I wasn't the sorority type. I'm just not cut out for throwing myself at frat boys and treating everyone else like dirt. And this week totally confirmed that for me. Maybe I needed this experience to find out who I am. Or at least who I'm not."

"But Val, you can't quit now!" Chloe insisted. "If you give up, then you're just letting Lindsay and Johanna win."

"I don't think so," Val reasoned. "I'm still the winner here. I mean, I did get in, didn't I?"

"Yes." Chloe groaned impatiently. "That's what I've been saying."

"So I did win," Val argued. "I got accepted as a Theta. I fulfilled my dream. But in the process I realized that the reality didn't live up to the fantasy. I don't need to be in Theta to feel important, to feel involved. They're no better than you or I, Chloe. They're just different. And I know for a fact that I'll have more fun finding my own friends—friends like you—than trying to fit in with a bunch of snotty sorority sisters."

Chloe was finally willing to accept that Val was serious. And she wasn't going to change her mind. In a way, Chloe did understand where Val was coming from. For one thing, Val really wasn't Theta material. She was too sensitive, too thoughtful. Val dealt with people on her own terms, not based on someone else's rules or expectations.

And Chloe had to admit, the pledge process did make her own stomach turn on more than one occasion. She knew that all the pledge requirements were established for a reason. But she agreed with Val that certain sisters had taken things too far. But then again, those sisters had been punished, hadn't they? And Val and Chloe were accepted because they stood up to them. So things had to be changing for the better.

Still, Chloe couldn't quite get over the thought of joining Theta without Val. She glanced over at her friend, imagining how devastated she must be by everything that had happened. Getting kicked out, then reinstated, and then kicking herself out. Val definitely needed something to take her mind off this whole Theta

154

thing. And so did Chloe. She had an idea.

"Hey, Val, Jessica's having a big party at her house tonight, remember? We should totally go. I mean, even if you're not joining Theta, I'm sure Jessica would still want you to come."

"I don't think so," Val answered quietly.

Chloe looked at Val with concern. She didn't exactly look sad. Just tired. "Oh, come on, Val, let's go. It'll be fun. Besides, it'll help us forget about all this pledge crap."

"No," Val insisted wearily. "You go ahead. Have fun without me. You'll be okay."

Chloe looked at her skeptically. "You sound so pathetic. Just come with me."

"No, really, Chloe, I just don't feel like a party tonight. Especially one that's sure to be filled with Thetas."

Now that Chloe thought about it, probably a lot of Thetas would be there. After all, it was Jessica's party. But that didn't bother her. Chloe still wanted to be a Theta. Didn't she?

"If you really don't want to go, I'm not going to twist your arm." Chloe sighed. "I guess I'll just have to go myself."

"You should just go, Chlo, really," Val insisted, heading for the door. "I know you'll have fun. I'm just going to go back to my room and study or something."

Chloe relented. "Okay. Well, see ya."

"See you later," Val added cheerfully as she made her way out into the hall.

As soon as Val was gone, Chloe looked toward her closet. She wondered what a reinstated pledge should wear to a party at the house of the pledge-week chair. She envisioned herself arriving at the party alone, in her sexiest little black dress. Then her thoughts drifted to Val and Deena, eating popcorn in their sweats and watching a movie on the VCR. For some inexplicable reason, she yearned for the latter.

Chloe closed her closet door, grabbed the leftover pizza, and left her room. She walked around the corner to Val and Deena's room and knocked on the door. Val looked surprised to see her when she answered. "Oh, hey, Chloe, what's up?"

Chloe offered a shy smile and gestured with the pizza box. "Suddenly I'm in the mood to watch a funny movie and eat tons of popcorn," she announced happily. "Plus I've still got all this leftover pizza. So I was going to see if you want to go to the video store with me and pick out something to rent. Is Deena here? Maybe she'll want to join us."

"Deena's actually out on a date tonight," Val answered in a voice that said she could hardly believe it either. "Some guy from her American-studies class. But I'd love to watch a movie with you, sis."

156

Val stepped forward and threw her arms around Chloe. As they shared a warm, friendly hug, Chloe truly did feel that she had a sister in Val.

As Sam saw the happy couple moving toward the stairs, he knew this might be his last chance to confront Finn about seeing him at Frankie's. And to clear his name with Elizabeth once and for all. Sam wound his way through the crowd to intercept them at the base of the stairs. On the way over he nearly bumped into Todd Wilkins.

They exchanged nods, but right now Sam didn't have time to talk. Not to Todd, at least. Sam tried to look as casual as possible as he approached Elizabeth and Finn. Like he was just running into them at a party. Not like he was heading them off at the pass.

When Elizabeth noticed Sam coming toward them, she did her best to ignore him. It was obvious she didn't want him talking to Finn. But Sam was not to be ignored.

"Hey, Wakefield," he said pleasantly. "Some party, huh? I never realized you guys knew so many people."

Elizabeth smiled nervously. "Yeah, I wish I did know this many people. But you know how parties are, especially when they're off campus. Suddenly everyone's your friend."

Sam glanced at Finn and lamely attempted a smile. "Hey, speaking of friends," he said pointedly. "You're Finn Robinson, right? I think we met a few weeks ago, when you were picking up Elizabeth for a date or something."

Finn smiled like a champ. "Yes, I think we did. You're Sam, right? I'm sorry, I don't recall your last name, Sam."

"It's Burgess. Sam Burgess. But just Sam is good enough."

"All right, Sam. Well, it was nice running into you again." Finn reached out to shake his hand in a combination of hello and good-bye. He nodded toward Elizabeth and again toward the stairs.

Elizabeth was practically tugging at his arm to drag him away.

But Sam wasn't letting them off the hook so easily. He held on to Finn's hand and studied his face. Like he was trying to remember something. "Hey, Finn, this is going to sound a little nutty, but didn't I see you at Frankie's the other night?"

Finn looked surprised. For a split second a hint of nervousness bled through his cool exterior. But of course he made an instant recovery, pulling his hand back from Sam's and playing dumb at the same time. "Nope, I don't think so. I don't think I know anyone named Frankie."

Sam chuckled. "Oh, no, Frankie isn't a guy. It's

a bar, Frankie's. You must know the place. It's way off campus, off Lincoln Avenue."

Finn acted as if he was racking his brain to remember the place. "Nope, buddy, can't say I've ever heard of it. Definitely haven't been there. I tend to hang out near campus, mostly where the other med students go."

He had Finn, and he knew it. And he was going to catch him up somehow. "Are you sure you've never been there? Because I could have sworn I saw you there the other night."

Finn was clearly impatient with Sam's line of questioning, but he still managed to stay calm. "Well, you must be mistaken, Sam, because like I said, I've never even heard of it."

"No, I'm sure I saw you there," Sam insisted. "You were with this smokingly hot blond chick, sitting in a corner booth. I swear it was you."

Finn laughed again. "Sorry, man, but I definitely would have remembered that. You must have seen someone who looked like me."

"Yeah, maybe you have an evil twin or something," Sam answered, with barely a hint of humor in his voice.

"Whatever, Sam," Elizabeth cut in sharply, grabbing Finn's arm to lead him upstairs once and for all. "If you're through with your interrogation, I think we're going to go now."

Man, this guy's good, Sam thought. He was

about to concede the round when he remembered something. Todd! Wilkins had been at the bar that night too. And Sam had just seen him at the party. If only he could get Todd to back him up.

Sam quickly glanced around. Luckily he noticed Todd standing a few people behind him, and he was just within reach. "Just wait a second, guys," he said to Elizabeth and Finn. "Todd was at the bar that night too. I wonder if he'll remember you."

Sam reached behind him and grabbed Todd's shoulder as Finn and Elizabeth let out exasperated sighs.

Finn crossed his arms against his chest as Sam dragged Todd into their conversation. "Hey, Todd, wasn't this guy at Frankie's the other night? I remember you were clearing, like, drink after drink from his table."

Todd barely acknowledged Sam and Finn as he came over and first said hi to Elizabeth. She offered a distracted hello, obviously aching to get herself and Finn away from Sam.

Sam rephrased his question to Todd. "Remember this guy from Frankie's the other night? He was sitting in that corner booth?"

Todd gave Finn a quick once-over and shrugged. "Man, I have no idea," he said to Sam. "Uh, no offense, dude, but there are just so many people in and out of there every night that it's hard to remember every face, you know."

Finn flashed a smug smile at Sam. He uncrossed his arms and held out his hand for Elizabeth. Elizabeth grasped his hand, and the two had begun up the stairs when Todd stopped them.

"Wait a second," Todd blurted out at Finn. "Now I remember. You *were* in the corner booth. And you were playing around with a stethoscope on a really cute blonde. Oh, yeah, now I totally remember you, man. I was wishing I had a prop like that for dates."

Elizabeth's jaw dropped and her eyeballs ballooned at Todd's revelation. She turned her head to face Finn and glared expectantly.

Yes! This was exactly the moment that Sam had been waiting for. Finally Finn was in the hot seat. Remarkably, though, he kept his cool.

"Sorry, fellas." Finn tried to sound friendly, but Sam could see him clenching his jaws. "Like I said, I haven't been to Frankie's in years. But whoever you saw that looks like me sounds like a real player."

"Yeah, he *is* a real player," Sam said suggestively. "I bet he has tons of different girlfriends."

Finn kept smiling. "Well, if you'll excuse us . . ." Finn turned to Elizabeth and tried to speak softly. "Elizabeth, why don't we *not* continue this discussion at *my* place."

Elizabeth managed a weak smile and redirected her glare toward Sam. She pulled Finn's arm around her, and the two of them headed for the door.

Chapter Twelve

Todd shrugged off his weird encounter with Sam, Elizabeth, and the mystery man and headed toward the kitchen to grab another brew. At least Elizabeth was too preoccupied with her little love triangle to have a chance to ask Todd any probing questions about his life. Or to be more precise, his life as Elizabeth imagined it: school, Dana, his apartment, and work. In that order.

Getting judged by his ex-girlfriend from high school wouldn't have been fun. But then again, he wasn't exactly having fun trying to talk to the snooty SVU girls at this party either. At least Elizabeth knew him. They had been close once, so in a way it was okay for her to judge him. Elizabeth had more to go on. She knew some history.

But these other girls were all about the present.

Their own artificial little world of SVU. Todd was surprised that most of them had even ventured the three blocks away from campus to come to this party. Every conversation was the same.

First she asks what my major is, then what frat I'm in. Then when I tell her I live off campus, she asks what kind of car I drive. Then she goes on and on about her sorority as if it's the epicenter of the universe. And anytime I mention Frankie's, it's like, "That townie bar? You work there?"

What a bunch of snobs, Todd thought as he looked around the living room. And then, as if to drive his point home, he spotted Lucy, the last SVU girl he had dated. And the last girl who had dissed him.

They had gone out to dinner the week before at a fancy Japanese restaurant. Everything had been cool—except for Lucy's slightly annoying habit of speaking exclusively on the subject of SVU sororities and fraternities—until Todd started talking about Frankie's. Then Lucy accused him of becoming a townie, like it was the same thing as joining the trench-coat mafia. Luckily tonight she chose to ignore him.

Now I'm definitely leaving, Todd resolved. He was about to forget the beer and head for the door when a beautiful black girl in a tight green dress and knee-high boots stepped in front of him and smiled. "Hey, Todd."

"Nina?" he asked, almost choking on his beer. He was unable to believe this hot girl was Nina Harper, Elizabeth's superstudious best friend. "Wow, you look really amazing. I almost didn't recognize you."

"You mean outside of the library?" Nina joked. "You probably just didn't expect to see me at a party."

Todd was surprised at Nina's familiarity with him. Now that he thought about it, the few times he had met her with Elizabeth, Nina had seemed kind of standoffish, way too serious about every little thing. All she ever did was study. Physics or something brainy like that. He figured that's why she didn't make a big impression on him before. But now she was making a tremendous impression. Not only was she incredibly beautiful, but she was also giving off a very sexy vibe.

"Last time I heard, you were dating Dana, right?" Nina asked.

"Yeah, I was," Todd answered cautiously, slightly taken aback. "I can't believe you remember that."

"Well, Elizabeth probably filled me in on the details," Nina answered, obviously trying to downplay her knack for recall. "I mean, I know you guys used to go out, right?"

"Yeah, but that was a while ago," Todd replied

wistfully, unsure of where Nina was headed with her questions.

"I'm sorry. I'm not, like, prying into your personal life too much, am I?"

Todd felt his face turning red. "No, it's cool."

"It's just that I don't really know anyone here, so it's nice to see a familiar face. So how is Dana?" Nina eyed Todd pleasantly. She definitely wasn't hitting on him, he realized. She was just making conversation at a crowded party.

"Oh, we broke up a few weeks ago," Todd answered, catching a tone of regret in his voice. "But it's all for the best. You know, things just weren't working out."

"Oh, I'm sorry," Nina offered sincerely. "But like you said, it's probably for the best. And I'm sure you'll have no problem finding another girlfriend."

"Yeah, I guess," Todd answered weakly. He wondered if Nina was available. "So, what's new with you?"

"Oh, so much!" Nina gushed. "I'm having so much fun this semester, it's crazy!"

"Really? Wow." Todd was intrigued.

"Yeah, I'm having like a Nina renaissance. No more endless nights in the library for me—no, sir. I've been going out a lot, seeing a lot of live music. Really living, you know? Not just studying all the time."

"That sounds cool," Todd answered, envying Nina's new lease on life. "So, what kind of music?"

"Well, my friend Francesca goes out with this guy who's in that band Wired. Ever heard of them?"

"I think so . . . ," Todd answered uncertainly.

"They play at Starlights all the time—they're really good. Anyway, I've been checking them out mostly." Nina paused. "And now I'm sort of seeing their lead singer. His name's Xavier, and he's totally amazing. In fact, I just came here with him, so he's around here somewhere. . . ."

Nina began looking around the room, evidently distracted by Xavier's absence. *Great,* Todd thought, *even Nina's having more fun than me.* "That's great, Nina," he answered with as much enthusiasm as he could muster.

Nina returned her attention to Todd. "So, what have you been up to? You must be doing something to keep yourself occupied. I never see you around campus anymore."

Todd was glad to finally have the chance to talk about himself. And to someone who wouldn't judge him so harshly for turning into a "townie." For a moment he had been feeling sorry for himself. Hearing Nina go on and on about all the good times she was having made him feel like he was somehow missing out on something. But when he thought about it, he had been having good times too. Just not around SVU.

"Well, I've got my own place off campus now," he began proudly.

"That is so cool," Nina enthused.

"Yeah, and I'm only going to school part-time now, which is probably another reason you haven't seen me around much."

"Part-time, huh?" Nina sounded intrigued. "So what are you doing with the rest of your waking hours? Do you have an internship or something?"

Internship? Todd didn't have time for any internship. He wasn't the type of gullible college student who would give his labor away for free in the name of gaining experience. No way.

"I've got this great job, actually," Todd boasted.

"Really?" Nina leaned closer. "Tell me about it."

"Well, it's at this bar, Frankie's," Todd explained. "It's kind of far from campus, so I doubt you've heard of it. But it's really cool, and all the people who work there are really great."

Nina took a small step backward at the mention of Frankie's. "Frankie's—isn't that a townie bar? You work *there*? Why?"

Todd took one last look at Nina and shook his head. It wasn't even worth explaining to her what was cool about his job, or the rest of his non-SVU existence, for that matter. She would never understand. For a minute there, Todd had thought Nina was different from all the other snobs at SVU. But now it looked like he was wrong about her.

He guessed he didn't belong at this party after all. Where he really belonged was Frankie's. With his real friends. Todd turned from Nina without saying a word and walked to the front door.

Elizabeth stared out the passenger window of Finn's Saab as he quickly took the turns on the winding road to his apartment. The night was clear and almost moonless, and the stars were out in merry company. *I really know nothing about the stars,* she thought to herself, staring evenly above the line of the trees. *They all have names. Names I don't know.* But they seemed like the best friends she had at that precise moment. At least she knew she could count on them.

How could Sam try that lame stunt again, and with Finn right there? Elizabeth felt that she had never been so embarrassed in all her life. *First thing tomorrow,* she resolved, *I am going to the off-campus housing office and looking for a new place. Because this is just too much!*

She didn't look over at Finn, just continued to gaze at the restful lights glittering in the endless black night. *No*, she thought, Sam *is going to find a new place. Why should I have to move just because Sam is losing his marbles completely?*

Sarcasm was one thing, mixed messages, the awkwardness of living with an immature boy. Those she could handle, and Sam's iconoclastic style of humor could be funny sometimes when he wasn't trying to ruin her life with it. But there came a point where you had to draw the line. Neil would back her up, she was sure, and so would Jessica. That was one of the advantages of being a twin. Jessica would always be on her side.

Elizabeth felt a twinge of guilt somewhere in her mind. She was sure Jessica would understand her reasons for wanting to kick Sam out, but Elizabeth wasn't sure that her sister would understand why she hadn't told her about the whole mess earlier.

Why *hadn't* Elizabeth told her about Sam's outrageous accusation right when he had made it? Why hadn't she told her what she was going to do *tonight*, or what she was planning on doing, or what she was thinking about doing anyway? Except she wasn't thinking about it—she was thinking about Sam. Why did she let him get to her! And why didn't she talk to Jessica sooner?

Elizabeth groaned inwardly. Stupid *Cosmo*

advice column. It was easy for Jessica to tell Elizabeth not to sleep with her boyfriend. She didn't have to carry her virginity around with her like a basket of eggs, always afraid of dropping it.

But it never was like that for her, Elizabeth admitted to herself. *Because she knew what she wanted. And when the time came, she didn't drop the basket. She just made it disappear and never looked back.*

Jessica wasn't the type to overthink, Elizabeth reflected. She never seemed to look back too much at what she might have done or what she should have done. What's done is done, she would say. *Well, not for me,* Elizabeth thought. *For me what's done is never just done. There's always a morning after.*

Still, she wished she had Jessica's perspective with her right now—brave but not reckless, and always with Elizabeth's best interests at heart. If Jessica hadn't looked at Elizabeth's quandary from the point of view of what Elizabeth really felt, maybe that was because Elizabeth had never taken the time to really tell her what she felt. Elizabeth experienced a pang of regret. Now it was too late.

Finn turned the car onto the tree-lined avenue near his apartment. They passed a little bar on the corner, neon signs blaring against the quiet night sky. A couple in evening clothes were out walking, hand in hand. They looked like they might be medical students.

Quite a different situation from that bar of Sam's, Elizabeth thought. *And Todd's. Todd is working there now!* Elizabeth was too upset to think very much about it, but the picture of her housemate and ex-boyfriend hanging out together at some way-off-campus bar gave her pause. What a world.

"I'm sorry about Sam, Finn," Elizabeth offered for the third time since they'd left the party. "Maybe he's just trying to protect me or something. He has a pretty warped view of human nature: All men are dogs. So he doesn't like you."

Finn smiled graciously. "I guess his heart's in the right place. He's just watching out for you." He reached over and patted her knee.

Elizabeth was impressed by Finn's magnanimity. He was so mature! "Well," she said, "I don't care for it at all. He wasn't too big on my being protected when it was *him* that my friends thought I needed protecting *from.*"

"What's that?" Finn asked concernedly.

"Oh, last summer we were on a cross-country contest together. There was a brief time when I thought there might be something possible for Sam and me, just for a little while, if you can imagine. How stupid! And then, like I couldn't handle *Sam,* two ex-boyfriends had to practically drag him off me. One of them was there tonight, actually. Todd. You just met him."

"You and *Sam?*" Finn repeated incredulously. He looked a little scornful. "Well, that explains everything! And now you live with him? Liz, what were you thinking?"

"I know," she admitted ruefully. "I was just thinking about how I have to get him out of the duplex."

"You can't let a loser dork like *Sam* think he has a chance with *you,* Elizabeth! Once he thinks that, there's no way he's ever going to let another man get close to you. You're the best thing that would ever happen to him in a million years! Now he's like a dog protecting his meat. Oh, this is rich."

"Yeah, well, he *is* childish."

"Childish is one thing," Finn declaimed. "Slander is another. If he wasn't a friend of yours, Elizabeth, I'd have let him have it right there. Like I would ever go to Frankie's, that scum pond!"

"Well, it was pretty strange that both Sam and Todd insisted they had seen you there," she murmured, not sounding confrontational, just perplexed.

Finn steamed. "Elizabeth," he said, "I have never been to that bar. And if I did go, and I can't imagine why I would, I would never bring a woman there. Never! And if, for some completely unimaginable reason, I did that, I would never play doctor the way those two guys said. I don't know what they put in the beer in that sleaze shack, but your two friends are nuts if they think they saw me there on a date!"

The car was approaching Finn's apartment, and Elizabeth just looked at her hands when he parallel parked. "I don't know why Todd would say something like that either," she intoned weakly. Why did she have to feel so unhappy?

"Didn't you just tell me that Todd did the same thing with you and Sam on the cross-country trip? The guy's obviously got some kind of complex about you. He needs to think of you as helpless. Trust me, I learned all about this in psychology. It's all in his mind! He doesn't feel good about himself, so by making you seem weak in his mind, he gives himself a sense of purpose. And when Sam comes up with this little scheme, Todd just goes right along with it."

Is that anything like projective anxiety? she wondered. She put that out of her mind and riffled through a set of mental snapshots of Todd. That didn't sound right about him. He had been pretty protective of her when they were going out too, she considered. And that was for a long time. And he had never seemed too insecure either. Quite the contrary. But then, that was before they started college. Things got different fast in college. Why *was* he working so many hours at Frankie's? It seemed out of character. *Oh, who knows what's going on with Todd,* she decided. *It could be anything.*

"So," Elizabeth said to Finn, "if you wouldn't take a date to Frankie's, where would you take her? The no-tell motel?" She was teasing. In the quiet car, in the dark, she felt like a weight had been lifted from her stomach.

Finn slammed his hands on the wheel. "Why won't you believe me?" he demanded.

Elizabeth gasped at his sudden display of emotion. "I was just kidding, Finn!" she protested. "I mean, where would your *evil twin* take her?"

Finn turned impassively to her. "I don't know any evil twin," he said. Then he reached over and took her hand. "But if there is another guy out there who looks like me, all I have to say is, he'd better keep away from you. 'Cause this town ain't big enough for the two of us."

Elizabeth was pleased by his tone. She felt truly safe with him.

Finn continued now, softly. "You're very special, Liz. A special, special young woman. I am so *honored* that you are going out with me, I don't even know how to tell you. I wish I could tell you how much you mean to me. But I can't. It's too hard. All I can try to do is to show you."

He squeezed her hand and looked directly into her eyes, then continued. "I promise you, Liz, I would do anything to make you happy, and I would never let anything bad happen to you. You've got a lot of friends, and I'm sure that their intentions are good. But those little boys don't know anything about real love, the love of a man for a woman, the love I feel for you with all my heart. Liz. I love you. I do. I love you so much. I don't want anything to come between us, not anything. We're together now, and that's the way it was meant to be, and that's the way it's going to stay. You hear me? No Boy Scouts or imaginary bimbos are going to get in the way."

Elizabeth listened to his avowal with increasingly passionate tenderness. How could she have listened to Sam for even a moment? This was a man, a real man, not one of Sam's imaginary dogmen. This was love, true love, not the heedless rush of one of Jessica's instant flings. This was the real thing, the love of a man and a woman for each other. She felt like the whole world was withdrawing from her, that there was nobody but herself and Finn, and nothing in the world but the two of them and the stars in the sky.

It's time, she thought. *It's time for the love of a man and a woman for each other to be made real. This is it. It's real. It's me. Finn and me. Now.* She felt the softness inside her sweetly as a shy smile grew across her face.

"Finn, darling," she whispered to him, running her hand along his thigh. "Can we go inside now?"

He didn't say anything, just opened the car door, walked around, and opened the door on Elizabeth's side. She lifted her hand for him to take, and he closed the door behind her when she stood up.

In the darkened avenue, under the starry sky, they kissed. Elizabeth felt her lips crushed against his like velvet. Their lips parted, their tongues touched, and Elizabeth bit him ever so softly on the corner of his mouth. Finn let his hand linger on her every curve as he slowly caressed her body. She shivered externally, but on the inside everything was on fire. She felt so soft. Everything was perfect. "Finn," she whispered in his ear. "Inside, now."

He took her by the hand, and they walked to his door.

Chapter
Thirteen

Sam didn't feel much like dazzling the ladies of SVU after all. Ever since Elizabeth left with Finn, he couldn't stop kicking himself. Kicking himself for letting them get away without forcing Finn into a confession. Kicking himself for being stupid enough to even think he could get a confession out of him.

And kicking himself for being so misguided as to even care in the first place. Now Sam was the one who looked like a jerk.

Obviously his attempt with Anna to teach Elizabeth a lesson about guys like Finn had failed miserably. *And Finn is probably sweet talking Elizabeth into his bed right now. Maybe Elizabeth was right,* Sam thought. *Maybe I am an ass.*

But he wasn't a liar. The way he'd gone about confronting Finn might have been wrong, but

Sam was still right. He *had* seen Finn at Frankie's with another girl. *Finn is a dog. And he's the one who's a liar,* Sam insisted inside his head. But Finn was still the one alone with Elizabeth. And Sam was the one alone with himself. At least that's how he felt.

Sam looked around at all the people dancing, talking, flirting, and having fun at the party. Everyone was having such a good time. Well, everyone except for Todd, who Sam saw bolting for the door with a sour look on his face. But aside from Todd, it was all smiles wherever he looked. How could they all have it so easy when everything was so difficult for him?

And what was he thinking anyway? How could Sam be in the middle of a great party full of cute girls—right inside his own house!—and still feel so isolated and depressed? Once again he kicked himself. But no matter how many times the big, imaginary shoe went *pow!* on his big, imaginary butt, Sam still couldn't shake the feeling of utter hopelessness when it came to Elizabeth. Why did he keep trying to get through to her? Why didn't he just follow Anna's—and Elizabeth's—advice and mind his own business?

Too many questions, Sam thought. *And not enough answers.* Sam looked down at the half-finished bottle of beer in his hand—his first of the night—and realized that he was no longer thirsty for a buzz. He wanted a clear head. And he wanted to be alone. Too bad his house was full of drunken idiots. *Maybe Todd had the right idea. Maybe I should just take off too.*

"Hey, Sam, why the long face?"

Sam looked up to see Neil with a concerned look in his eyes.

"Oh, nothing." Sam looked down at his feet. "Just stuff. Hey, what's up with you, Neil?"

"Just meeting and greeting," Neil answered with a playful touch of irony. "You know me, ever the happy host."

"So who was that hot young scholar with the cool retro clothes I saw you talking to earlier?" Sam asked, in a concerted effort to be social.

"That was Jason," Neil answered with a sly smile.

"The guy from your poli-sci class?" Sam asked.

"Mm-hmm," Neil purred. "Problem is, Jessica seems to like the guy too. You'd think she'd trust my gay radar at this point, but she's insisting the guy's straight. She's way wrong. Hey, let's go find him so I can introduce you."

Sam raised his hand in a tired protest. That sounded much too complicated for his brain right now. "You know what, Neil? I should probably meet him another time. I'm not really in the mingling mood right now."

"Evidently," Neil answered dryly. The look of concern returned to his face. "Is there anything I can do?"

"No, I think I should probably just go chill in my room." Sam sighed. "Alone."

"Suit yourself, Sullen Sam," Neil huffed, and then added, "but seriously, if you ever want to talk about anything, I'd be happy to listen."

"Hey, thanks." Sam put his hand on Neil's shoulder. "I'd like that. Maybe tomorrow, after I've had some time to think this through on my own."

"Okay, Sam. You know where to find me." Neil gave Sam a parting wink and walked across the room to greet a group of people that was just arriving.

Sam returned to his bedroom and shut the door behind him.

Nina silently shook her head after Todd walked away in a huff. What was his problem? *And what's with the townie fantasy he's so caught up in?* she wondered.

I guess we're all changing, Nina mused. *Todd's turning into a townie, and I'm suddenly partying and dating a musician. Hey, where is my musician?*

Nina glanced around the living room for Xavier, who had split off to mingle the moment they walked in the door. Nina wondered where he was, and for a moment she worried about all the attractive women who were no doubt throwing themselves at her date right now. But then she caught herself and remembered what Francesca had told her about guys in bands. Nina only wished she felt as secure about Xavier's feelings for her as Francesca did about Billy.

Nina made her way to the kitchen to find herself a drink and look for Xavier. Every step she took through the crowded party, she could feel guys staring at her. Now, this was a new experience.

As Nina approached the counter where drinks were being made, she was overwhelmed by the vast array of liquors and mixers, wines and beers, and half-empty cups strewn about. She wasn't much of a drinker, and she didn't quite know where to begin.

"Can I help you?" A muscular, dark-haired football type in a tight, black, ribbed T-shirt held an oversized bottle of vodka in one hand and half a lime in the other.

Nina was surprised at being waited on. "Oh, are you the bartender?" she asked with a shy smile.

"I am now."

"But you're not, like, working here or any-thing . . . ," Nina offered tentatively. She hadn't been to that many parties and wasn't exactly sure how it worked with the drinks and everything.

"Well, no," he replied, as if the idea were preposterous. Then he added with a warm smile, "But if you'll allow me the honor, I would be happy to be your personal bartender for the evening. My name's Lawrence."

Nina shook his extended hand and noted his quick glance down and up the expanse of her body. "Nina Harper. Nice to meet you."

"So what can I get for you, Nina Harper?" He beamed.

Actually, you could find my boyfriend for me and send him right over, Nina thought. But somehow she didn't think that line would fly. Besides, Xavier would be along soon enough. In the meantime she would enjoy the kindness of strangers. A drink to start and hopefully some scintillating conversation to follow.

"Well, what are *you* drinking?" she finally asked.

"Greyhound," Lawrence answered smugly. "Vodka and grapefruit juice. How does that sound?"

"Sounds good to me, I guess," Nina answered with a giggle.

"Nina, leave the driving to me." Lawrence expertly poured a splash of vodka at the bottom of a tall plastic cup, dropped in a few ice cubes, and filled it nearly to the top with fresh-squeezed grapefruit juice from a plastic container. He then added a small slice of lime and a wedge of lemon.

"Here you go—one Greyhound à la Lawrence." He handed Nina the plastic cup. "The lemon and lime are my own special touch."

"Thanks, Lawrence." Nina took the drink and raised it slightly in a gesture of appreciation.

"*Salud!*" Lawrence raised his own plastic cup and clicked it against Nina's. "To your health. And might I add, you do look very healthy. If you don't mind my asking, how do you keep in such great shape?"

Is he talking to me? Nina asked herself. She couldn't remember anyone asking her for fitness advice before. Not that Lawrence needed any.

"It seems to me that I should be asking *you* that question," Nina answered shyly. "Just about the only thing I do is walk between my dorm room and class, and to the library and back. You, on the other hand, obviously spend a lot of time working out."

"Well." Lawrence feigned modesty as he glanced down at his bulging chest and biceps. "I've definitely done my time in the weight room. I guess I do it because it helps relieve stress."

185

"It does more than that," Nina marveled. "You've really got a great body."

"Thanks." Lawrence smiled at the compliment. "Hey, do you wanna go out back and get a little air?"

Nina hesitated. *Gosh, one innocent compliment about his physique and he's asking me to get some air with him? What is that, a code for going to make out? Isn't this a bit abrupt?*

Nina wasn't quite used to house-party chitchat. She guessed she had better watch what she said lest certain people think she was leading them on. In the meantime she had better stop Lawrence right in his tracks.

"Actually, Lawrence," she said with a friendly smile, "I should probably go find my boyfriend. I think he's in the living room."

"Right on." Lawrence was unfazed by her sudden departure. "Well, it was nice talking to you. And enjoy that drink, Nina."

"Thanks, I will." Nina turned and headed for the front of the house.

As she entered the living room, she glanced around for signs of Xavier. Unfortunately he was nowhere to be seen. She had been standing alone for barely thirty seconds when a cute, hip-hop-looking white guy with blond hair, oversized jeans, and a backward baseball cap approached her.

"Hey, aren't you in my journalism seminar?"

"No, I don't think so," Nina answered without having to think about it.

"Are you sure?" he asked, scrutinizing her face. "You look really familiar."

"Well," Nina began with an amused smile, "since I'm not even taking journalism, I'm fairly certain that I'm not in your seminar."

"Oh, my mistake," he apologized. "Maybe it's some other class."

"Yeah, or maybe you've just seen me around campus or something," Nina offered graciously.

"Right, that's probably it." He nodded and extended his right hand. "By the way, my name's Charlie. What's yours?"

"Nina. Nice to meet you."

"Yeah, me too." Charlie held her hand for a second longer than usual for an innocent greeting. "So, what classes *are* you taking?"

Her school schedule was the last thing Nina felt like discussing right now. And even though Charlie was cute and nice, she didn't feel like wasting any time on small talk right now. Especially when she knew that Xavier was somewhere inside this house.

Besides, there seemed to be no shortage of good-looking guys wanting to talk to her tonight. Nina was amazed at all the boys who were checking her out and approaching her. It kind of felt weird. But she had to admit, she loved the attention!

It's like a tight dress and knee-high boots are all it takes to change your life, she thought. *Now, if I can only find the guy I had in mind when I put this outfit together!*

Nina spotted Jessica across the room—an easy excuse to extricate herself from Charlie. "Um, excuse me, Charlie, but I see someone I really need to talk to."

"Okay, well, uh, I guess I'll see you in journalism, heh heh."

Nina rewarded Charlie's lame attempt at humor with a small courtesy smile and quickly walked the other way. As she made her way toward Jessica, Nina wondered where Elizabeth might be. She was looking forward to meeting Finn, especially now that she knew he was The One. She knew he was going to be at the party, but now she was beginning to think that the two of them had already left. A curious smile crossed her lips. *I wonder if tonight is The Night.*

Todd gave the empty Coke can another good, hard kick down the block. He'd been kicking the same can for twenty minutes, ever since he'd left that stupid snob-fest.

Isn't that a townie *bar?*

You work there?

Omigod! Like, aren't you totally afraid of getting, like, beat up?

When had they all changed? Todd wondered. The people he used to hang out with had once been so cool. Now they were just a bunch of stuck-up jerks who thought they were better than everyone else.

I'm so great! I'm an SVU student! Mommy and Daddy pay for everything and even send me an allowance! Me, work? Hel-lo!—how would I keep up with my studies?

Ugh. Even thinking about the typical idiots at SVU made Todd's stomach feel queasy. But the long walk home was doing him good, he realized as he turned a corner and finally let the can go.

You've moved on, he told himself. *It's not that the people you used to hang out with have changed. It's that* you've *changed.*

And he was doing exactly what he'd set out to do. Live like an adult. Be on his own.

He walked faster, suddenly having a destination other than his lonely apartment. He'd go to Frankie's, where he belonged. Where people made him feel good about himself.

He saw the orange footsteps on the sidewalk and followed them around the corner to the bar. Peering in the window, Todd could see the little

189

nightclub was hopping. He smiled. The place was packed with so-called townies who looked like they were having a lot more fun than the snobs at the snob-fest.

Todd pulled open the door and headed inside. He'd see if Rita could use his help tonight. If not, Todd would hang out as a customer. He was going to drink, dance, and have a blast.

Just like the rest of the townies.

Finn turned on the hall-light switch. Tiny rainbows danced across the walls. Elizabeth propped herself up by her hand on the sideboard and reached down to undo the straps of her heels. But before she could, Finn slid his arm gently around her waist, held her close to him, and kissed her neck.

Elizabeth felt the blood rushing to her head. Her hand trailed in the air as he scooped her up in his arms. She let her head hang back, her blond hair swinging to and fro in the soft light.

Shadows hugged the high beams of the ceiling. Finn kissed her neck passionately, holding her in his arms by her back and legs, his easy strength and sweet caresses a pleasure to her. Turning slightly, he carried her into the large apartment.

Elizabeth sat up in his arms, her wrist around

his shoulder, and clung to him. He felt so strong where he held her, at the backs of her thighs and under her shoulders. Through the tiny skylight she saw a few stars twinkling. *Hi, guys,* she thought. She nuzzled his neck with her lips and then sucked it gently. *My darling,* she thought.

Finn walked with Elizabeth in his arms over to the bed. Supporting her weight and kissing her softly, he sat down on the edge of the broad futon and held her closer to him. She kissed him softly, tenderly, warmly taking each lip into her mouth and caressing it with her tongue. His kisses were like sugar to her, and he stroked her shoulders and calves with his soft hands. She felt the world slipping away.

This is how it should be, she thought, relaxing under his sweet touch. She kissed him without stopping, the hot, wet mix of their mouths growing tempestuous between them. *And that was when I knew,* she thought. Reaching down to her ankle, she tried again to undo her shoes.

"Mmm, don't," Finn said, holding her errant hand in his. "Leave them on."

She giggled. Kinky doctor! When his hands slid up the back of her leg, though, she gasped with pleasure and desire. *Oh, yes, yes, yes,* she thought.

Turning with her in his arms, Finn gently lowered her down to the bed. Her hair spread out beneath her on the coverlet, and she felt the smooth softness of the material on her bare shoulders. Her feet dangled over the floor. Taking his arms in her hands, she pulled him down to her.

Again they kissed, Finn's hot tongue probing deep in her mouth. Elizabeth ran her hands over his taut shoulders to his neck and then ruffled his hair. Finn slid his hands underneath her back and legs again and lifted her above the bed. She rested her cheek on his. Carefully walking on his knees on the bed, he lowered her down again, in the center.

Elizabeth felt her heels catch on the bedspread, and then she was half sitting, half lying on the bed, Finn's arms around her, the skirt of her dress sliding up her legs to her hips. Gently Finn lowered her head to the bed, kissing her all the time.

Suddenly there was a stirring beneath her, slowly at first, and then a cat jumped out from underneath her body and scampered away. Elizabeth giggled. She had almost crushed him. Finn seemed startled by the cat and knelt stiffly above her as the gray tabby ran around the apartment, settling on the floor by the sink. "Since when do you have a cat?" she asked, surprised.

Finn stood up off the bed and walked over to the kitchenette. "I promised a friend of mine I'd take care of him while he was away for the weekend. Maybe if I feed Mr. Pookie, he'll keep off the bed."

Elizabeth laughed, watching Finn pour dry cat food into one bowl and water into the other. "That ought to hold you for a while, Mr. P.," he said, reaching down to give the cat a quick stroke as he ate. Turning back toward her, he walked to the bed.

Elizabeth caught a half glimpse of his broad shoulders as they were momentarily caught in the light cast by the prisms, all colors sparkling briefly over his shirt and then dark again as he stood beside the bed with her on it. She wanted to feel those shoulders bare under her hands.

"Finn," she purred. "Take off your shirt."

Finn's hands went to the buttons of his cotton Brooks Brothers oxford. Elizabeth's eyes were adjusting to the dark, and she watched with pleasure as he stripped it off.

"Here, let me help you," she said. Rising to her knees, she scooted over to the side of the bed.

Finn pulled out his shirttails and tossed the shirt over the side of the chair. He stood beside her, and she was almost as tall as he, kneeling next to him on top of the bed. She kissed him hotly, first on the neck and then the shoulders, and then down and down along his firm chest. A little fine hair lay between his hard, flat pecs. Elizabeth slowly dragged her tongue over his smooth skin, pushing her lips harder and harder against his gorgeous body, moved with passion and desire.

She held his upper arms in her hands, her face buried against his chest. He sighed and groaned as her lips and tongue circled over his breast and then settled themselves on his neck.

Completely lost in the moment, she could feel Finn's hands rapidly moving over her back. Slipping them both over the backs of her thighs, he grasped her to him suddenly and lifted her upright off the bed. With her head now higher than his, she kissed his lips from above.

Finn eased his grip slightly, and her body slid against his until her heels again rested on the floor. She felt a burning desire deep within her beneath his hands, where they held her, where her back had rubbed against them as she slipped through his warm embrace. She wrapped her arms around his neck again and kissed him dizzily.

Elizabeth felt Finn's hands exploring the back of her dress. Fearlessly she imagined the buttons that ran up the back of the dress as Finn's hands rested on each one, his nimble fingers leaving them open one by one. The dress loosened around her shoulders. This time she didn't stop him.

She thought about the bra and panties she wore underneath, chosen specially for tonight: pink silk with tiny red bows. He held her to him tightly. She felt the warmth of his skin against hers and clung to his back. "Oh, Finn," she whispered, "oh, Finn, oh, Finn."

Chapter
Fourteen

Nina stood talking to yet another cute guy in the succession of cute guys that had been approaching her at the party all night. She was still basking in the glow of all this newfound attention but couldn't help yearning for that certain singer with whom she had walked in the door more than an hour before.

Finally she felt the familiar touch of his strong, gentle hand on her hip from behind. "Hey, buttercup," Xavier growled in her ear.

Nina felt a warm, gooey, trembly sensation expand from the pit of her stomach and spread throughout her body as she turned her head slightly to brush her cheek against Xavier's smooth, full lips. She turned her head back to face the well-heeled blond boy behind her, and the edge of Xavier's mouth lingered for a moment on the side of her neck.

The preppy stiffened in acknowledgment of Xavier's special place in Nina's world. He mumbled something about getting another drink and quickly slunk away, leaving Nina and Xavier for a proper greeting—after what felt like so much time apart.

Nina put her arm around Xavier and traced the muscular contours of his back with her bare, open hand against the luxurious black silk of his simple, elegant shirt. She moved her hand down and rested it with her thumb tucked suggestively into the waistband of his dark brown cords. He touched her waist again and pulled her toward him. Nina adjusted her hands to appreciate the parts of his body where chiseled chest met washboard stomach beneath his shirt. They kissed briefly, without tongues, and then locked their eyes in a passionate, thoughtful gaze.

At last Xavier broke the spell with his words. "So when do I get to meet Elizabeth?" he asked, conveying an interest in Nina's life without sounding impatient.

"I don't know." Nina frowned slightly. "I haven't seen her all night. I'm thinking she maybe took off with her boyfriend before we got here."

"Oh, I didn't know Elizabeth had a boyfriend," Xavier remarked.

"Yeah, Finn," Nina answered. "Elizabeth is

crazy about him. He's in SVU med, so he lives in the med-student dorms near the hospital. That's probably where they are now."

"Hmmm . . ." Xavier placed a thoughtful hand on his chin as a mischievous sparkle glinted in his eyes.

"What?" Nina insisted with a big, suggestive smile.

"Oh, I was just thinking. . . ." Xavier paused, tilting his head and narrowing his eyes. "If Elizabeth isn't home, perhaps you and I could go up to her room for a little privacy. Do you think she'd mind?"

A butterfly leaped inside her stomach as Nina considered the proposal. She looked up at Xavier and could hardly believe she was standing so close to him. That she was actually *with* him. And that *he* wanted to get even closer.

He's so sexy and cute. And caring and nice. So smart, so different from everyone else. Not to mention he's the lead singer in the coolest band. He could have any girl he wants. And he wants me!

Nina thought back to the hours they spent backstage at Starlights. The memories of the green couch had flitted in and out of her mind so many times since then. And she was aching to create some more memories—to fuel her thoughts when Xavier wasn't with her.

She figured Elizabeth wouldn't mind, as long

as they didn't make themselves *too* comfortable in her bed. But was Nina really ready to be alone with him? Even though this was only her second night out with Xavier, she already felt so good about him, about *them*. Everything felt so right. So real.

She guessed that it would be okay to fool around a *little*. After all, there'd be lots of time to get to know each other later.

"I don't think Elizabeth would mind at all," Nina finally answered with a sly smile. She offered her hand to Xavier and led him toward the stairs.

Elizabeth and Finn were in a hot embrace on his bed, kissing furiously, their hands exploring the warm curves of each other's fully clothed bodies. He was going slowly, she realized with pleasure. Her dress was still on, although it now draped low on her shoulders.

He's not rushing me, she thought. *He's trying to make me comfortable. And it feels so amazing . . .*

He lay next to her on his side, leaning his torso over her. Then he pressed the full weight of his chest against her. She could feel his passion stirring, and she hugged him closer to her, their kisses growing more passionate. *All right, now,* she thought briefly, the weight of the moment edging into the corner of her consciousness.

Elizabeth realized that Finn was undoing his belt.

Loosening it. Unbuckling it. Pulling it off and tossing it to the floor.

She lay still on her back and turned her head to the side reflectively. Time seemed to slow down. She was acutely aware of the feeling of the bedspread on her bare back and legs.

Somewhere Mr. Pookie was drinking out of his water dish, his ID tag jingling against the metal bowl. Her blond hair, mussed on either side of her, tickled her nose. Elizabeth raised her eyes up to Finn's dark figure.

He wasn't unzipping his pants, she realized with relief. She needed just a little more time to get used to his belt being off. A little more time to get used to lying on his bed. He stroked her hair and kissed her neck, not furiously, but sweetly. Tenderly. Exactly as she needed him to.

It's as if he can read my mind, she thought. *That's how strong our connection is.*

She sighed contentedly. She was surprised by her own sense of calm. Where was her terrible anxiety now? She smiled to herself. *It really isn't such a big deal.* She would be so relieved when it was finally over. The burden of protecting her virginity seemed like a distant, nagging task. And now she would be done with it. This was love, real love, the love of a woman for her man. The distractions of her uncertainties seemed a thousand miles away.

Uh-oh, birth control! Suddenly the image of the condoms and the set of pills in her purse popped into her mind. She bit her lip.

Why had she brought those pills along? They were pointless. She wasn't even going to be able to start taking them until her next period, and it would still be another month after that before they were effective. And the condoms! When were they going to discuss his sexual history? Not now! How could she deal with this without ruining the mood?

"Finn," she whispered. He didn't pause from the trail of kisses he was making up her neck.

She could feel one of his hands slide away from her as his trail of kisses continued. *He's unbuttoning his pants,* she realized in panic.

He's unzipping his pants.

He's trying to shrug out of his pants and kiss me at the same time.

He's flinging his pants to the floor.

Suddenly she felt the taste of fear in the back of her throat. And it had only a little to do with the fact that Finn hadn't brought up the subject of birth control or his sexual history.

It was simply fear. *What happened?* she wondered frantically as his kisses now trailed across her shoulder. With his mouth he eased the neck of her dress down a bit, and his lips blazed a fiery path. Why was she freaking again?

He lifted up a bit, then laid his torso against her completely, his hands pushing down her dress. He toyed with the strap of her bra.

This has to stop before it's too late!

Uh-oh, Nina thought, eyeing Elizabeth's perfectly made bed as Xavier made a diving leap onto it.

"Comfy," he said, patting the blanket. "Come sit next to me, Nina."

Maybe this wasn't such a good idea, after all, Nina thought. What if Elizabeth came home unexpectedly and found her best friend and some strange guy in her room? Nina knew she herself wouldn't appreciate a couple fooling around in *her* room, on *her* bed. She'd totally freak out, and she knew it.

But this was sort of a special occasion. Just because of *who* Nina was with. Xavier wasn't just any guy. And besides, it wasn't as if Nina were going to sleep with him, or anything. Just make out, fool around a little. Maybe just snuggle.

"Ni-na," Xavier sing-songed, stretching out on the bed. "I'm a little lonely over here."

Nina smiled and slowly stepped to the bed, admiring his incredible body as she sat down on the edge. She could barely take her eyes off of him to remove her shoes.

"Good idea," Xavier said, sitting up to remove his boots."

Strains of a rock song floated up through the floor, and the only illumination was the moonlight barely lighting up the window. The darkness, the soft music, the romantic quality of Elizabeth's attic room . . .

He cupped her chin in his hand, turning her face to him. Gently, he pulled her close. Closer. Closer.

He kissed her.

Softly. Tenderly.

Then harder.

Nina wrapped her arms around his broad shoulders. She was lost. Lost in how this felt, lost in how *she* felt.

Lost in being wanted by a guy like Xavier. No, not *like* Xavier. Xavier.

Suddenly the door opened. Nina shot up.

That had to be Elizabeth!

Nina's heart was beating a mile a minute. Elizabeth would not appreciate this. Not one bit. And what if she had Finn with her? Some embarrassing first meeting this would be!

Giggle. Giggle-giggle.

No. Not Elizabeth, Nina realized. Even Elizabeth in love would not giggle, let alone giggle like that. That giggle had "Use me, I'm a drunk freshman" written all over it. *Giggle*. *Giggle*.

Nina breathed a sigh of relief. It was a girl and a guy, both seniors, actually, poking their heads through the door. "Oh. Guess this room's already occupied," the guy said with a laugh.

"Let's just hang out in the hall up here," the girl told him. *Giggle*. *Giggle*. The door closed behind the couple.

Behind her on the bed, Xavier sat up and wrapped his arms around her neck, gently tugging her back down. "See, everyone's got the same things on their minds tonight," he whispered in her ear. "Being alone with their sweeties."

Am I your sweetie? Nina wanted to ask, not even sure what "sweetie" exactly meant. To him, anyway. Did it mean "significant other?"

"Xavier," Nina said. "I'm not too sure we should be in here. I mean, I feel sort of cheesy for using my friend's room like this. I don't think she'd like it. It's not cool at all."

"Nina, baby," he said, trailing a line of kisses across her arm. "If it's not us, it's those two who just left or some other couple. Better you, a friend of hers, than some strangers who wouldn't even bother making the bed after."

After? Nina wondered. After *what?* She wasn't going to get *under* the covers with Xavier yet.

205

He found her lips with his own, and in mere seconds, Nina was once again lost.

You're in love, Liz, Nina thought, *so you'll forgive me.*

How can such a loud sound come out of such a small girl? Chloe wondered, trying to ignore Val snoring away on her bed. And how could anyone fall asleep during *Dirty Dancing?* Chloe had seen the movie at least ten times and could see it ten more times.

Chloe reached for the remote control and lowered the volume. She peered over at Val, lying on her stomach on her bed, and then clicked off the VCR. Today had been an amazing day. Val could probably use the sleep.

And I could use a party, Chloe thought. *I'm a Theta! And I'm going to Jessica Wakefield's tonight!*

Chloe stretched, then hopped off Deena's bed and smoothed the comforter. If Deena, of all people, was out on a date, then Chloe should certainly be able to *get* a date. And she wouldn't get one by hanging out in a dark room with a sleeping best friend on a Saturday night!

Quietly pulling open the door, Chloe turned out the light and slipped out of Val's room. She ran down the hall to her own room.

Moira, thank God, was out. Probably tormenting

some freshmen to make up for the humiliation she'd suffered during pledge week. Never in a million years would Chloe let Moira forget that she had seen Moira cry. *If*, that is, Moira ever tried to torment *her*, again.

There was nothing like having a little power.

Anyway, she'd soon be free of Moira Pierce. Soon enough, Chloe would be installed in the Theta House, her new home. She'd have a new roommate, new friends. Sisters.

College would be everything Chloe had dreamed it would be.

Chloe opened her closet and rooted through her clothes, looking for the perfect outfit for tonight. Jessica knew a ton of people, and so did her housemates, so Chloe was sure to meet at least a few eligible boyfriends at the duplex.

Grabbing a tight black sweater, black stretch pants, and her high-heeled black leather boots, Chloe took off the sweats she'd worn for the movie-fest and then changed into party-wear.

Not bad, she thought, examining herself in the mirror. She slicked on a little brownish lipstick, blotted her lips, and kissed her reflection.

Time to go meet a guy to like!

Chloe grabbed her little purse with the long shoulder strap, slung it over her chest, and headed out. She practically ran the almost-mile to Jessica's house.

She could hear loud music the minute she'd turned the corner onto Crescent Road. A million cars lined the streets, and it seemed like tons of people were coming and going from the house.

This party was going to be great!

Chloe headed up the walkway, smiling at the group of four guys who were walking in. They smiled back.

Tight black sweaters always seemed to have that effect on guys.

She followed them inside, feeling herself getting even more psyched by the booming music, the shoulder-to-shoulder people filling every possible inch of space, the loud voices, and the laughter.

This was a party.

Chloe craned her neck to seek out Jessica. She looked around for the blond head, but there were so many pretty, slender girls with straight blond hair in the living room and hallway that Chloe couldn't tell if any of them was Jessica.

"Hey, Chloe."

Chloe whipped around to see Neil Martin, one of the cutest guys she'd ever seen in her life, smiling at her. Of course, he was gay. The one incredible-looking guy who was actually nice to her was totally unattainable!

"Have you seen Jessica?" Chloe shouted

over the music. She stepped back to let a group pass by.

"Yeah—kitchen," Neil called back. "We're gonna head out to Starlights and go dancing in about a half hour. Wanna come?"

Chloe beamed. "Yeah!"

"Cool," he said. "If we miss you when you leave, just meet us there, okay?"

Chloe smiled and nodded. Her life was changing already. She was a Theta. She was at *the* party of the semester. And she'd just been invited to hang out after-hours with the cool people!

Chloe caught a glimpse of Lila, Alexandra, Denise, and a bunch of other Thetas sitting on the sofa and on the coffee table. *Those are my new friends*, she thought happily. *I'm one of them now!*

She was about to join them when she was tapped on the shoulder.

"Hi," said a male voice.

Chloe turned around to see a somewhat nerdy guy smiling at her. He had curly light brown hair, brown eyes, eyeglasses, a slightly big nose, and he was wearing what her mother would refer to as *slacks*.

"I'm Martin," he said, sticking out his hand.

"Uh, Chloe," she told him.

She had to shake this guy. He was *not* eligible boyfriend material.

"I know this is gonna sound like a line," Martin began, "but, you have the prettiest eyes I've ever seen."

Chloe tilted her head and regarded Martin. "Um, thanks," she replied. No one had ever said that to her before. She'd been told she was cute, even pretty, but no one had ever just come out and told her she had the prettiest *anything*.

"I guess you hear that all the time, huh?" he asked. He shifted his cup from one hand to the other. *He's nervous*, Chloe realized. *I'm making a guy nervous!*

"Well," Chloe murmured, "I suppose I do hear it a lot. I mean, from guys. But I appreciate it every time."

Martin smiled—nervously. "So, can I get you something to drink?"

He was looking at her so hopefully, Chloe couldn't say no. Plus, now that she was getting used to how he looked, she was realizing that he wasn't *that* nerdy looking.

"Okay," she told him. "Why don't we head into the kitchen? My friend Jessica's in there, so I'm dying to go say hi. She's one of the people who lives here. Which one invited you?"

"Don't tell anyone," Martin whispered in her ear, "but I sort of crashed the party. I heard about it and figured who'd know I wasn't invited? And I was right. Everyone just figures someone brought me or invited me."

This Martin guy is my kind of person, she realized.

"Pretty smart," she told him, smiling. "That's something I'd do!"

Martin beamed. "Shall we?" he asked.

"We shall."

As Chloe led the way to the kitchen, she was aware of Martin behind her, watching her, probably even admiring the back of her head.

So what if he's a little nerdy? she told herself. He's nice, almost sort of cute, and he likes me. Plus, he's definitely got *some* degree of coolness if he crashed the coolest party of the year.

"You know," she said as they weaved their way through throngs of people toward the kitchen door. "Some friends of mine are heading to Starlights in a little while. If you're in the mood to dance, why don't you come?"

"I'd love to," he said.

Chloe beamed for the hundredth time in the past ten minutes.

Chapter
Fifteen

"Finn," Elizabeth said, more clearly this time. "Darling. Stop."

Finn rolled off her and lay beside her body, his lips lingering over her ear. "What is it?" he whispered, kissing her softly.

Elizabeth couldn't bring the words to her lips. She recalled what the counselor had told her at the clinic. "We . . . we have to be careful, right?" she whispered nervously, the subject of birth control the only reason she could come up with at the moment for stopping him.

She felt Finn's face pull sharply away from her ear. "Of course we do, darling," he whispered. "Of course." He sat up and opened the drawer of his night table. She heard him rummaging through its contents. Her eyes trailed up to the skylight. *Hi, guys,* she said to the stars. *I hope you're watching over me right now.*

Finn pulled a roll of condoms from the drawer, set them on the table, and then lay back down beside her. "Don't worry, darling," he murmured. "We'll be protected."

Elizabeth felt her throat constrict. Now what was she supposed to say?

This was a big mistake. This was going completely wrong. All the security drained out of her. "No," she said. "I . . . I . . ."

He was kissing her neck again, but she was insensitive to his touch. "Finn," she said.

"It's all right," he said between kisses. "You have nothing to worry about, Elizabeth. I promise."

"I . . . I need a glass of water," she told him. "I'll be right back." She hopped from the bed and straightened her dress as she hurried to the kitchen.

"Hurry, gorgeous," Finn murmured from the bed.

She turned on the faucet and stared at the running water. Suddenly all she wanted was to be home, in her attic room, listening to Jessica ramble on about the latest issue of *Cosmo*, even listening to Sam go on and on about Playstation. Anywhere but in Finn's bed with a roll of condoms on the table next to him.

What happened? she wondered again. *I thought I was ready. I was ready in the car. I was ready when*

I walked through the door. I was ready when I let him lead me to the bedroom. Why aren't I ready when it comes right down to doing it?

Why am I so terrified? She realized it wasn't the same fear she'd felt so many times, afraid that she didn't know what she wanted or that she would regret her decision later. This was *outright* fear, a cold, prickling sensation all up her spine and down to her fingertips.

It's not time for me. Not yet. This is not right. She realized that the fear she felt was fear that it would be too late to stop, too late to reconsider. Finn walked into the large room and stopped to pet Mr. Pookie, who lay contentedly by the entrance to the kitchen. "You must be really thirsty," he joked, gesturing at the running faucet.

She quickly shut it off, glad to be able to turn away from him for the moment. It wasn't too late to stop, she realized. It was never too late to stop if that's what you wanted.

And she wanted out.

Finn walked into the kitchen and took her hand, kissed it, then led her back into the bedroom. She followed him, not ready to speak yet, not ready to tell him that she still wasn't ready. She wanted just a few minutes more of—*Of what?* she wondered. Of his thinking they were going to make love? Of his happiness at the idea? Of his approval?

He laid her down on the bed, then stretched out next to her, stroking her shoulder, running his finger down the center of her dress to her belly. He might as well have been measuring her for clothes. The desire was gone from her, and so was the pleasure. She felt herself hardening inside, and suddenly the quiet of the dark room felt oppressive. She had to get out of there and now!

"Finn," she said. He wasn't listening. His hands caressed her tummy, and then his other hand began pulling down her dress. Elizabeth sat up quickly. "Finn, stop. I'm not ready. Oh, Finn, I'm so sorry. But we have to wait."

Finn snatched back his hand. "All right," he said. "No worry, Elizabeth. We've got all night." He snuggled closer to her. "I know exactly how you feel, you know? Remember, it's our first time for me too. We just have to take it nice and slow. I'll be so gentle, you won't believe it. And you'll feel so good, I promise. Everything's going to be all right."

But this wasn't what Elizabeth wanted to hear. "No," she insisted, softly but firmly. "We have to wait. I'm sorry, Finn, but this isn't going to happen tonight."

"What's wrong, Elizabeth? I thought we settled this."

"We did," she said. *No, actually you did,* she thought. "But it's just not right. Don't you understand? I want my first time to be something really special. I don't want it to happen when I'm not feeling ready. It can't be special that way."

"This is special," he protested. "Liz, how long do you want me to wait?"

"I don't know," she said. "But it has to be like this. I'm sorry. Can't we just snuggle and go to sleep?"

"Go to sleep?" Finn asked incredulously. "Maybe you can, but I sure can't. You get me so worked up—look at me." The foil-wrapped condom sat in his hand. His bare chest and legs suddenly seemed bizarre to her. She felt like a child. "Elizabeth," he said. "I have to have you. I love you, Liz, and I need you. Completely. Totally. And right now."

He rolled over on top of her, his face buried in her neck, his hands gripping her by the legs, pressing himself into her body. Elizabeth felt a horrible emptiness surrounding her. Why wouldn't he stop? She froze beneath him.

For a minute longer Finn remained on top of her, wiggling, trying to kiss her. But Elizabeth was like a stone.

"Finn, stop!" she cried. "Stop! Now!"

His head darted up and he stared at her, then he rolled off her. He stood up, took his shirt off the floor, and put it on, leaving it unbuttoned. "You know," he said, "you are really something. You have really gotten me all turned around."

Elizabeth felt sorry for him. She had to admit to herself that her feelings had been running very hot and very cold. "I—I'm sorry, Finn," she stammered. Why did he have to seem so angry? "I know what I said—and look, I meant to go through with it tonight. But now I just can't. I know how you feel. But I told you, it has to feel right, or I'm not going to . . . to . . . I'm just not going to do it!"

Finn smiled at her cruelly. *"Do it,"* he mocked. *"Do it.* You know, Elizabeth, sometimes you make me so tired. We're not kids! So you're late losing your virginity! So what? Why should I have to suffer? I've given you everything you want. Now how about me? How about giving me what I want?"

Elizabeth couldn't believe what she was hearing. "How do you know you've given me everything I want?" she asked accusingly. "You have no idea what I want."

"Yeah, well, right now, Liz, I really don't care. I am so sick of your little high-school games. You are such a tease. You know, your flirty little maybe games might work on your idiotic friends, little Sam the private eye and his moronic busboy sidekick Todd, or whatever his name is, but I'm sick of them. I can have any girl

I want, Liz, and I picked you. So you'd better get on the ball, girl, 'cause I'm sick of waiting for you to come around. It's got to be now or forget it."

Elizabeth was shocked beyond her ability to respond. He had never spoken to her like this before. She felt like she had been slapped. This wasn't the Finn she knew. The Finn she'd fallen in love with. This was someone else entirely. Someone she hadn't even known existed. What if she'd actually gone through with it? She didn't even know Finn Robinson!

"Well," she intoned icily, "maybe you are wasting your time with me. Because I'm not having sex with you. And if you can have any girl you want, why don't you go call your little blonde and take her back to *Frankie's*." The last word was like ice spitting out from her lips.

"You know," Finn said, "I just might do that." He walked over to his desk in his underwear and picked up the phone. Glancing down at his notebook, he dialed a number. Then with the phone in his hands, he walked back over to the bed, sitting beside Elizabeth and looking right at her. Elizabeth heard a woman's voice.

"Hi, Barbara," Finn said into the phone. "Oh, I'm all right," he said casually, reaching down to the floor for his pants.

Elizabeth shot up off the bed and buttoned

219

her dress. She felt nothing now but cold indignation, not embarrassment, but clear, incisive humiliation. Trying to walk to the bathroom with a semblance of dignity, she stumbled in her high heels.

"Yeah," she heard Finn's voice continuing, "I went to some stupid college-kids' party—don't ask me why. Oh, yeah, so boring. But you know who I ran into there? Some guy who works at that little townie bar we went slumming at the other night."

Elizabeth whirled outside the bathroom and faced him. So Sam and Todd were telling the truth! She hadn't even been serious when she'd mentioned Frankie's—it hadn't occurred to her to think he'd really been there with another girl.

She felt the pain and humiliation wash over her from head to toe. Finn looked right into her eyes and gave her a big wink. Then, with a dismissive gesture, he turned his head away from her and continued his conversation. "And that got me thinking, you know, what a good time we had. . . . Yeah, yeah, me too . . . so how about I pick you up in, oh, say, fifteen minutes?"

She stared at him, stunned.

"We still have time to grab a couple of rounds before last call," he said into the phone. "Sure, we can come back to my place after. I have those earrings you left here safe and sound in my bedside table." He hung up and smiled at Elizabeth.

"You bastard," she hissed.

"Yeah, well." Finn was pulling on his pants. He looked for all the world like he had never seen her before in his life. "That's the way it goes, Lizzie. I really liked you until you pulled this final act of little girldom, but all's fair in love and war. Now do me a favor, and call yourself a cab. I have a date in fifteen minutes. With a *real woman*," he added smugly. "A woman who knows how to treat a real man."

Elizabeth held her head high. She didn't feel sad or even hurt. Mostly she was just disgusted. Disappointed in herself, but disgusted with Finn.

"Well," she said calmly. "I hope she gets to meet one sometime." She marched to the hall, found her purse, and walked out.

The walk to the bar near Finn's apartment was long, cold, and torturous. Elizabeth felt herself falling apart one piece at a time. First the tears began to fall, dropping softly to the sidewalk. Then she felt her legs growing weak, and it was all she could do to keep going.

She felt so ashamed. Not of what she had done or of what she almost did. She was ashamed of having let herself fall for Finn's superficial charms. She felt a great, cold emptiness where her feelings for him had been, and as her mind traced over their courtship, the little things that she had found so delightful ebbed out of her mind one by one. Now she was overcome by disgust, and she felt like throwing up.

Perfect, she thought. *Just right—throw up too. And then what? Pass out on the street?* "Pull yourself together, Liz," she heard herself say softly to the breeze. And then she was at the bar, putting coins in the pay phone.

"C'mon, Jessica," she urged into the mouthpiece as the phone rang and rang. "Please answer, Jess, I need you so bad right now." The machine picked up, and she heard Neil's clear voice on the message. She yelled into the phone after the beep: "Jessica! Jessica! It's Elizabeth, Jessica! Pick up the phone!"

Nothing. Cursing her luck, she hung up and redialed. But as the phone rang, her tears exploded with a new force. She felt so alone. Now she wouldn't even be able to keep herself composed if some drunken idiot answered. And sure enough, a man's voice came on the line and sloppily said hello.

"Um, hello." She sniffed into the phone. "Um, this is Elizabeth Wakefield, and I live there?"

"Hold on," the voice said. She heard the phone being put down. *No,* she thought, *don't go get me—I'm not there! Why didn't I just ask for Jessica?* But then she heard a door close, and the room got quieter, and someone picked up the phone. "Elizabeth? It's me, Sam."

"Sam, I need to talk to Jessica, okay?"

"She took off with her Theta crew for Starlights," Sam said. "Neil and some guy went with them too. Hey, what's up with you? You don't sound too good."

Elizabeth silently calculated her options. She didn't know what to do. "Liz," he said, sounding genuinely concerned. "Is everything okay?"

"No," she said sharply, losing control of her voice. She was crying hard now. "No, everything is not okay. I—I—"

"Elizabeth, where are you?" he asked. "Just tell me where you are, and I'll come get you right now."

Elizabeth just wept, clutching the telephone up to her ear.

"Wakefield, are you at a party? I hear a lot of noise in the background. Just give me the address, and I'll come pick you up."

She shook her head.

"Elizabeth, I can't hear you. Where are you?" She looked at the sign above the mirror behind the bar. "L-L-Lucky's," she managed to say.

"Lucky's," he said. "That little bar by the med school?"

"Yeah." She barely choked out the word before racking sobs overtook her.

"I'm going to be right there. You just sit tight, okay?"

She didn't say anything. She didn't much want to see Sam. But what choice did she have? She could feel her legs wobbling beneath her. Propping herself against the wall, she burst into another round of tears.

"Liz, I'll be right there. Don't go anywhere."

Somehow Elizabeth managed to hang up and get herself over to a chair. She collapsed into tears, resting her face on her knees.

She could sense people looking at her, whispering and staring. After a moment she reached down, undid the straps on her shoes, and pulled them off. Holding them in her hand, she walked in bare feet out to the sidewalk in front of the bar and sat down on the curb with her shoes resting beside her. She laid her face down on her knees again and wept.

"I have two left feet," Martin said. "I'll just watch."

Chloe smiled and grabbed Martin's hand, practically pulling him onto Starlight's crowded dance floor just as the song ended.

"And now for all you love birds out there," the DJ announced. "A slow song for slow dancing."

Chloe looked at Martin. Boogying was one

224

thing. But slow dancing? That was something else.

Before Chloe could suggest heading back to their booth, Martin had taken her hand. He put his other hand on her waist and began swaying perfectly nicely.

She looked around; it wasn't as if anyone was watching them. Not that Chloe was embarrassed about being seen dancing with a nerd.

He's not that nerdy, she reminded herself. *He's just not . . . not . . . not that cool.* He's not the guy who Chloe had worked so hard to attract. She hadn't rushed and pledged Theta so that she could date a social outcast who couldn't get invited to parties!

Chloe heard Jessica's unmistakable laughter, and she glanced around until she spotted the blonde a few couples away. Jessica was slow-dancing with Neil, and they were laughing and talking.

See, she told herself. Neil and Jessica are just buds. It's not like one slow dance means you and Martin are like a couple, or anything. It's not even necessarily romantic. It's just a slow dance! It's no different than dancing with your uncle at a cousin's wedding.

Martin was smiling at her. He removed his hand from her waist to push his glasses farther back on his nose. "You have the prettiest hair too," he said.

Chloe beamed. "You're, like, the nicest guy."

"I am pretty nice." He smiled again. "You seem nice too."

"Me?" Chloe sputtered. "I can be, I guess."

That was weird, she thought. *Why am I suddenly being honest?*

Martin held her hand tighter. "So, um, do you think you might want to go out with me sometime?" he asked. "Like to dinner?"

Wow, Chloe thought. *I came to Jessica's party to meet an eligible boyfriend, and I'm actually being asked out on a date!*

But by Martin. Nerd.

He's not so nerdy! she yelled at herself.

One little date wouldn't mean anything. It wasn't like she had to commit to Martin for the rest of her college career. Plus, it would be good practice to go on a date with him. She needed to work on her skills for when the frat guys started asking her out.

"Sure, Martin," she told him. "I'd love to go out with you.

Sam conjured his video racing skills as he powered his clunky car through the tree-lined streets of Sweet Valley. Speeding toward the bar, he was glad he hadn't finished that first beer.

Elizabeth had sounded pretty desperate on the phone, and he wanted to reach her before she completely broke down. He only hoped she was all right. He knew she couldn't be doing that great if she had allowed him to be the one to come get her. (Really, he was the only one who *could* pick her up. He was just happy that the tipsy, lingering idiot who'd answered the phone had had the sense to tell Sam that someone was on the phone.)

As he turned the corner, the medical school loomed into view. Sam slowed the car and kept an eye out for Elizabeth. There she was, sitting on the curb in front of the tavern with her head buried in her hands, her shoes on the street in front of her. He eased the car to a stop and got out with the engine still running. Cautiously he walked up to where she was sitting. He could hear her muffled sobs and saw that her body was slowly convulsing.

Sam spoke tentatively, in the softest voice he could muster. "Elizabeth?"

She raised her head from her hands and exposed her red, puffy, tear-streaked face to the light of the street lamp.

Even though she didn't manage a smile, Sam had never seen her so happy to see him. He bent his knees and tenderly offered a hand under her elbow. He helped her up and kept his hand gently on her arm as he led her to his waiting car. For the first time in his life, he actually opened the passenger door first. She got into the car without speaking, and Sam walked around to the driver's side.

Once he was inside, Sam glanced over at Elizabeth to make sure her seat belt was fastened and then shifted the car into gear. He decided that she wouldn't be up for much conversation, so he kept his eyes on the road as he silently cursed Finn Robinson. *Liar. Dog. Predator. Skank.* Sam almost felt guilty himself for embodying the unsavory characteristics of Dr. Scumbag during his little charade the other morning. It really was a stupid stunt, he realized. Why didn't he just persist in telling the truth about seeing Finn at Frankie's until she finally believed him?

But of course he had tried. Over and over again, he tried. He had even confronted Finn with the incriminating information—and a witness! But Dr. Dog had just been too good—or too bad—to crumble under the pressure.

And Elizabeth had been so hopelessly in love with him that she was blind to the truth. *Blinded by lies* was more like it. And now Sam was left wondering what had finally turned her around. What had happened in that bachelor apartment to wake her up to the real truth about Finn Robinson? But the more Sam wondered, the less he really wanted to know.

More than anything, Sam was simply glad that

Elizabeth was okay. Or was she? She was pretty broken up when she called and didn't seem much better when he picked her up. And now she hadn't spoken a word since getting into the car. He wondered if she needed a real doctor. Or the police.

Sam decided not to take Elizabeth directly home. The party was still rocking—he was sure of that much. And the least he could tell was that Elizabeth wasn't in the mood for a big bash, especially one taking place in her own house.

He decided to pull over at a quiet lookout point. As Sam eased the car into a secluded spot overlooking the city, Elizabeth finally raised her head and spoke for the first time.

"W-Why are we stopping *here?*" she asked.

Sam answered calmly, "You definitely don't want to go back to the house right now. It's completely packed with drunk, noisy people. I thought we could just sit here for a while . . . unless you can think of a better place. And don't worry, you don't have to say anything if you don't want to."

A heavy silence lingered between them as Sam imagined Elizabeth trying to process the evening's events inside her head.

After a minute Sam added, "Unless you want to talk . . . in which case, I'm totally here to listen.

But don't worry about me. I haven't been drinking. And I'll spare you any of my patented Sam Burgess imbecilic remarks, I promise."

After a few minutes more she finally mustered the power of speech. She was no longer crying, but her voice cracked as she tried to speak. "You know, Sam"—she paused to blow her nose in a tissue—"you were totally right about Finn."

Sam breathed a silent sigh of relief, even though he hated the thought of Elizabeth finding that out the hard way. And he certainly wasn't looking for any validation right now. "I know, Elizabeth, I know," Sam murmured softly. "But listen, we don't have to talk about any of that right now."

After a moment more she added, "I'm just sorry I doubted you, Sam. I really had no right—"

"No, Liz," Sam interrupted. "Of course you had every right. I know I've been a total jerk to you in the past. And my credibility rating can't be very high with you."

"It is now," Elizabeth insisted, almost managing a smile. "Oh my God, how could I have been so wrong about someone I thought was so right!"

"Well, I'm not exactly Mr. Right," Sam admitted sheepishly.

Now Elizabeth really did manage a weak smile. "Not you. I was talking about Finn."

"Oh, I mean, duh . . . ," was all Sam could manage in response. *Stupid!* He silently chastised himself. *Can't you keep your foot out of your mouth for five seconds?*

At least his faux pas did something to break the tension in the car. But as Elizabeth began speaking—and sobbing—again, the tension rose back to critical levels.

"Oh, Sam, it was awful," she began. "I really came so close to actually sleeping with that jerk, and to think . . ." The words trailed off as Elizabeth broke down into a surge of tears, her body jerking with every sob.

Sam suddenly felt helpless. What could he say to make things better? What could *he* possibly do to comfort her? As if by instinct, Sam slowly reached over and put his arm around her, gently cupping his hand around her shoulder.

Elizabeth leaned toward him and rested her head on his chest. The hot tears flowed down her face and were absorbed by his shirt.

"Everything's going to be okay, Elizabeth. I promise." Sam could feel his heart constrict inside his chest. He squeezed Elizabeth's shoulder and held her tightly.

BFYR 232